Hermit Girl

E. M. Collyer

True, this is a work of worrying fiction. Any similarity between the ideas expressed herein and actual events should be considered extremely coincidental and the product of overactive imaginations taking pattern matching way too far. Stop it. Any similarity between the characters in this work and any persons living, or dead, or doing something in between, is to be expected. Let's face it, people aren't all that different. Let's not kid ourselves here.

Please do not copy or distribute any part of this publication. There's very little money to be made as it is. No part of this book may be reproduced in any form, or by any means, without written consent from the author, except in the case of short and rather wonderful quotes clearly attributed to the author. Thank you for your help.

The author has requested that ten percent of the profits of this novel be donated to the Children's Adventure Farm Trust - bringing love and laughter into the lives of children who have known too much darkness. We are more than happy to participate.

-- Left Field Books

Where to stalk E. M. Collyer on the internet:

thehermitgirl.blogspot.com

In the unlikely event that you don't thoroughly hate this novel and plan on burning it in a cleansing ritual (digital copies included), please consider leaving a review on Amazon/Goodreads/LibraryThing/etc. It goes a long way towards making future novels possible.

So I'm not one for complaining – okay I am, most of the time, but I'm not complaining right now, so bear with me – we really dropped the ball on this whole *life* thing. We did. All of us. By most estimations civilization has been going strong in some form or another for about six thousand years, but in all that time, did we find a cure for the most common of all human problems?

No, we did not.

In fact, we've collectively produced millions of books and movies about love and relationships, but is there even one well-researched tome on how best to *un*-fall in love? On how to instantly and effectively get over someone?

No, there is not.

The only thing out there is some lame advice on keeping your distance and giving it time. And maybe burning some photos while eating a particular kind of willow bark – and I'm not even sure about that one, I might've made it up.

But I'm going to back it up here a moment, Alice, because that's not really where I wanted to start. So many things have changed since you left, I'm so different from the girl you knew back when we were little, that I often wonder if you'd even recognize me now, and if you'd still want to know me.

So maybe I should start with the familiar. The few things that haven't changed. I still can't communicate with people. On any level. I still feel like everyone else shares this hidden, common language. This secret code that explains why they all get along so easily while I feel like an alien standing on the sidelines – someone who looks human enough, but who never quite fits in. And I'm still terribly, debilitatingly shy. That continues to be the proverbial wheel clamp on my almost non-existent social life. Yup, I'm still a raging extrovert stuck in an introvert's body!

Sometimes I think I'd rather die and be buried in a shallow, unmarked grave than talk to new people.

But, as I said, there are some things that have changed, and the biggest is definitely the fact that I had to deal with a breakup.

Yes, you heard right, Alice: your Willow had to deal with a breakup!

I know you won't believe me, so let me explain how I got into this mess in the first place…

1

I'm a bit like moss; at first you don't notice me, but while you're not looking, I secretly grow on you.

I'm clicking around my desktop aimlessly. I'm moving icons, opening tabs, and re-checking emails. Temp jobs are supposed to suck, I know, I'm not a complete moron, but mine sucks significantly more than the legal suck-able limit. I had to take matters into my own hands.

Clicking around my desktop isn't doing it for me, though, so I'll have to think of something else. Sadly, the corporate overlords have locked down all social media and blocked every single site that carries even the smallest amount of interesting information. So that's a dead-end.

Also, I've chewed on my pen about as much as both I and the pen can deal with, so I get up and peek over my cubicle wall. Maybe I can follow one of the other temps out to the coffee area. Not that I'll be able to interact with them, of course, or can even tolerate the taste of coffee, but if you're going to sneak off it's best to have a few people in your general vicinity to can act as a buffer.

No such luck, though. All the temps look suspiciously busy. Dutifully kneading their brains to fit that boring, corporate mold.

I quickly drop back into my seat when I spot Gary walking the floor. I can't let him see me.

Gary is our supervisor – a tall guy in his fifties with a thick mane of pepper-and-salt. You probably wouldn't call Gary a silver fox, but he does have one of those wise and friendly faces, like a younger, slimmer Santa. Don't be fooled, though. Gary's anything but friendly. In fact, he might be the only boss on the planet with a strict 'closed-door' policy.

One of the other temps rubbed him the wrong way on her first day – checking her cell during a meeting – and she's still licking her mental wounds from the aftermath.

So I wait a full five minutes before I peek over my wall again. (Only Biro and I know what happens during that time, and neither of us is talking). Gary has vanished. I sit back and breathe a little easier. I can finally open Keep and work on something interesting. Something of my own.

Keep is one of the few cool sites that the overlords have missed. Probably because it doesn't look like it could assist you in committing large scale time-theft. But it can, especially if you enjoy jotting down ideas for your YouTube channel.

I make it a point to write up any interesting thoughts that occur to me during the day, then I let them ferment until I come up with a fun little insight or an unexpected conclusion. Something that'll help me or people like me.

As I'm typing away, though, I notice a disturbance in the air. A tiny fluctuation of pressure that's accompanied by a whiff of what some people might call an appropriate aftershave for the workplace (those people would be wrong, though, terribly wrong!)

I just know it's Gary. I just know he's standing right behind me, looking at my screen, judging me.

My first instinct is to drop everything and run up to the roof and commit ritualistic suicide. Somehow, though, I manage to stay in my seat and take a deep breath. I remind myself that Gary has no idea that I'm working on a YouTube script. If he's even looking over my shoulder at all he'll just see a screen full of text. If I just alt-tab between applications as if I'm looking for something, then he won't catch on. He won't even have time to read my screen.

This'll work.

So I alt-tab my little heart out and land on my email application, which I left it maximized last time. It immediately fills my entire screen, blocking out my script completely.

Step one complete.

Now I'll turn as if I've only just realized there's someone standing behind me exuding cheap cologne at me, and all will be well.

This might actually a teachable moment, I decide. Fodder, perhaps, for a future video: getting caught is usually preceded by you acting nervous and guilty, it's almost never preceded by you looking cool and composed. Just pretend you're doing something completely normal and no one will ever figure out what you're up to.

"What're you doing?" Gary says, his voice gruff.

He was indeed standing in my cubicle 'doorway', and he doesn't look happy.

"Just working," I tell him. I can't read his expression but the fact that he's over fifty and not wearing glasses right now cements my belief that he hasn't seen my script.

I'm safe as houses.

He steps closer, torturing my nostrils with his aftershave. "I thought I saw you typing a large piece of text," he says.

"Might've been, sir," I say, feeling extremely uncomfortable in his gaze. "I was probably making notes on one of the quarterlies."

"No." Gary shakes his head. "You were typing something about '*cool guys*'."

My face starts to burn. "'Cool guys? I doubt that." I try to smile politely but I can't feel my face. I have no idea what it's doing right now. It's bright red, though, that's for sure. I can only hope Gary remembers that my face always turns red, not just when I'm guilty of Grand-scale Time Theft.

"You were," he goes on. "I definitely saw the words 'cool guys' as I walked by. Then I stopped and watched you type the word '*kissing*'."

I think my face is going to melt off.

"Perhaps you saw that wrong?" I stammer.

"No. You were definitely typing the word 'kissing.'"

"It might have been an elaborate typo."

Gary ignores me. "It made me wonder," he says. "It made me question exactly what kind of financial quarterly could necessitate the inclusion of the words 'cool guys' and 'kissing'..."

I can't answer because I can't talk. I can't even look at him. Seriously, why doesn't the ground ever open up and swallow me? There's like a million undiscovered sinkholes in the world, why don't I get one?

Gary leaves a thick, angry silence in the air as he turns to leave. "Remember," he says, "I still have to do the evaluation for your temp agency."

I wait until he's out of sight before I start breathing again.

No more slacking off today. No way. I turn back to my screen and close my script, then continue sorting quarterlies. And I don't look up from my work until it's well past time to go home – then I grab my coat and race for the door.

On my way home I detour to the mall to get some peppered Brazil nuts. Today there's only a single clerk on duty at the nut store and that's Somewhat-Square-Jawed Bailey – or SSJ Bailey for short.

I call this guy SSJ Bailey, not just because I'm too embarrassed to ask his name, but because he looks like a Bailey and his jaw is, you know, somewhat square. That is to say, it's square enough to be attractive while not being so square that he's too attractive to talk to. There is such a thing as jawline-overkill and Bailey's superior genetics have avoided this pitfall nicely.

I chose the name Bailey because I always think of Baileys as guys who have bright blue eyes that radiate mysterious wisdom, who often have quirky, casual hair that looks like it hasn't been checked in any kind of reflective surface in days, who are wiry without being too buff, and, when they smile, showing you that one tooth that's slightly out of alignment, you just know that something wonderful is going on in their cute, manly heads. Something way beyond our mere mortal realm.

Yup, I've got it bad.

"What'll be?"

I hesitate. Of course I do. Even though I knew this was coming, even though I came here specifically to see him (who eats peppered Brazils anyway?) I still fumble. I have my answer ready but when he looks at me my face starts to burn and my throat clams shut.

Honestly, I have dreams about someday being a normal person and just using my words to, you know, say stuff to people.

"250 grams of peppered Brazils," I finally manage.

I mumble, of course. I'm barely audible. But SSJ Bailey's smile doesn't falter. "Roasted?"

I nod.

"Would you like to make that five hundred grams? We have an offer."

He points out a flyer on the counter and I pretend to read it for a moment. It lists some inane restrictions that I have no hope of assimilating in a timely fashion. My brain just won't work right now, not with SSJ starting at me. So, to minimize the risk of looking even more dopey, I just shake my head. After all, my goal here is not saving money on nuts. The Brazils are going straight to the bin the moment I get home.

"No? Okay, no problem." SSJ Bailey gives me another quick smile, then disappears to the back.

My mind immediately relaxes. It goes all silent and tranquil like a deep lake somewhere out among ice and fjords. Wonderful. Yogi's would envy me. But I know it won't last. Not for long, anyway. As soon as SSJ Bailey returns, it'll go right back to high alert. Not in the least because of what I have planned next.

2

A test to see if He is the right guy for you:

Whenever something fun happens, do you think: I wish He *could see this? (1)*
Whenever you spot a beautiful cloud, do you think: I wish He *could see this cloud with me? (2)*

(1) Yup, he could really be the one.
(2) Stop it! You're being a big sissy! It's just a cloud!

Way before I'm ready for it, way before I've even caught my breath let alone caught my brain, SSJ Bailey returns with my order.

"Anything else?" he says, weighing the Brazils and bagging them up. "We have a new consignment of smoked almonds. People seem to really like them."

This is the moment I've been waiting for. This is where I dazzle him with a cool, well-crafted line that shows him how smart and funny and wonderful I (probably) am. Basically my next line will showcase my entire personality in all its complex glory.

So here it goes.

I force myself to look up at Bailey, to actually make eye contact, but then, for a long moment, I'm completely mesmerized, my mind ingesting the little details: the way his hair hides one of his eyebrows, the shape of the birthmark on the side of his nose, that bit of crust caught in his eyelashes, his mouth opening, showing his beautiful teeth, with that one tooth slightly out of alignment, and him saying, "Hello? Miss? Do you want to try the almonds?"

I wrangle myself back down to earth. "I... erm... I was..."

A groan rises from the line now forming behind me. Try as I might, I can't remember what I was going to say. My brain is completely stuck. I don't even remember what language I was going to speak.

"Are you okay?"

"I'm fine," I manage. "Don't worry, everything is okay."

This is terrible. I can't have him questioning my mental health. Not now. Not when I'm only just starting to act weird.

"I have my Brazils," I say, trying to buy time, hoping my brain'll get back into gear. "So, well, I guess that means I'm set."

"Great." SSJ smiles and moves over to the register to ring me up.

Even with everything that's going on I still notice that his current smile is particularly nice. Really special. I wonder if maybe this is not a professional smile at all. If maybe this is a personal smile. One that he's created especially for me. Now that would really be something.

I make a mental note to find out if there's a way to tell the difference between a professional smile and a personal smile. Perhaps Google knows. If not, it'll go onto Keep and I'll investigate it myself. This is an important skill to develop and share on my channel.

SSJ Bailey hands me my change and I quickly search for something more to say, something fun and quirky. Something so cool he'll simply have to remember me – specifically as someone he'd like to hang out with. Soon.

Sadly, by the time the transaction is complete my brain still hasn't shifted into gear and I have no option but to thank SSJ for his impeccable service and be on my way.

The day doesn't get any easier, though. There are no points awarded for suffering. The moment I get home Mom fills the air between us with a dense stream of complicated questions that need immediate answers.

"Why are you late?"

"I'm not. Almost to the microsecond this is the time I come home every day."

"It's almost dark."

"That's just what happens this time of day. I have no influence."

Mom's not having my sarcasm. "Where did you go?"

"I didn't go anywhere, I just stopped by the mall."

"What do you need to go to the mall for?"

"No reason. I just had to pick something up."

Mom shakes her head. "I really don't understand why you can't come straight home if it's dark. You know there are rapists all over the place and you should be tidying up the house instead of making yourself available to rapists."

"I'm not making myself *available* to rapists," I point out. "And the rapists don't care, anyway. They've unanimously decided that I'm not pretty enough."

Mom doesn't skip a beat. "They rape ugly girls too you know. Don't think they don't."

"Gee, Mom, I was kidding, but thanks for running with the whole ugly thing."

Mom waves it away. "You're not ugly, and I wish I could find a way to make you see that one day. But you know what I meant. It's not safe out there."

I hang my coat, give Mom a kiss, and head up to my web-studio.

As hard as it is to believe, apparently Mom wasn't always like this. My aunt tells me she used to be this happy, funny, carefree woman. Often the life of the party. Which is near impossible to imagine. Sadly, one day, when I was around nine, she suddenly changed.

I can't say I remember Mom ever being happy or carefree, to me she's always been the way she's now, but I wish I could go back in time and meet that other Mom. I'd love to talk to her, see what she was like, laugh and cry with her, and maybe find out what made her so afraid of the world.

I enter my little studio and boot up my laptop. Our living arrangements are somewhat strange, I'm fully aware of that. In fact, I was all set to move out after college, even found a couple of places around town that would suit me, but then Mom and I realized that the cost of living would actually go up for both of us. Also, I'm not sure what would happen to Mom if I moved out. I don't think it would be anything good. So, instead, we set up an agreement.

So even though it might look like it, I'm not still living at home. I just share a place with a roommate who's a little older than I am and who happens to share fifty percent of my DNA.

That's all this is.

I close my studio door and take a few breaths. I have to reorient myself because the second most important part of the day is coming up. (After the part where I drive ten miles out of my way to, apparently, embarrass myself in front of SSJ Bailey.)

3

I have to focus and get into the Zone. I'm about to create a new video for my channel.

It's important to keep updating your channel or whatever modest following you've gathered will dissipate. Even when you don't have much to say, you still have to go out there and say it. Saying nothing in an interesting way is still preferable to saying nothing at all.

But I always do my best to a least present a new take on things, a different way of looking at the world. This means I spend a fair amount of time going through my notes on Keep before deciding on a topic. When I've found something good, I write up a script to keep me on track during the take, and then I dig out my art supplies to whip up some old-school presentation cards.

I know that last bit sounds very macaroni-and-glitters of me, but bear with me, there's science behind his. (Science that I made up and never double-blind tested, but science nonetheless.)

It's easy to add a PowerPoint slide to a video or to spice things up with fancy animations, but if you make your cards by hand and hold them up to the camera you'll leave a much deeper impression.

Think about it, people are used to seeing professionally edited presentations. You can talk about any topic while showing a beautiful animation depicting the lifecycle of a turd and no one would bat an eye. Our brains are trained to assume presentational graphics make sense so we simply ignore them. They're invisible to us. That's why even a badly drawn card is preferable. The brain sees it and goes: *'Shoot! What's that really badly drawn card doing there?'* And – presto! – it's paying attention.

Told you there was science behind it.

It's the same with guys, when you think about it. Sometimes you just have to jump out of their PowerPoint world and make them sit up and notice you.

I make a few more edits, then head down for dinner.

As per usual, Mom has many questions about the world that only I can answer.

Mom: How was work?
Me: Work was work.

Mom: Did you finally make some friends?
Me: Friends? I'm surrounded by corporate drones and corporate drone wannabees, there's no way I'm making friends at that place.
Mom: Nonsense. That's just something you tell yourself because you're too scared to talk to them and find out what they're really like. You should ask one of them over sometime. Whatever happened to that Mandy? Why doesn't she come round anymore?
Me: She moved away last spring, remember?
Mom: Oh, right. Well, what about Susan?
Me: Mom…
(That's right, both my childhood friends moved away and in the same month, more or less. We keep in touch through email from time to time but those times appear to be moving further and further apart.)
Mom: What about that Melissa girl from down the street? You liked her, didn't you?
Me: You mean Melissa Moretti? Her family moved when I was twelve. Last I heard she was running some import/export business overseas.
Mom: You should look her up.
Me: I'm not sure that'd be a good idea. I think the only thing she liked about me was that we shared an unhealthy attachment to Tamagotchis. I doubt we could connect over that now. Anyway, I'm far too busy with my channel. It's finally taking off.
Mom: Didn't you say you only had five followers?
Me: Maybe. Could be. But everyone knows getting those first five followers is the hardest. Getting five followers is basically the definition of it taking off. It starts the ball rolling. Word of mouth. Recommendation engines. It's all lining up.
Mom: So when are you going to line up a boyfriend?
Me: How I'm supposed to find any kind of boyfriend if I can't even go to the mall after work?
Mom: Of course you can go to the mall, just don't go at night. Anyway, the mall is no place to find a quality boyfriend.
Me: So where are all these quality boyfriends who never go to malls?
Mom: I'm glad you asked. I was talking to Maureen and she mentioned her cousin is still single.
Me: No. I'm not going on a blind date. No way.
Mom: Then you'd better call and cancel.
Me: Cancel? You made a date for me? How can you do that?
Mom: It wasn't that hard. She asked if you were free on Saturday and I said yes. Presto, you have a date.
Me: I can't go. I'm way too busy! I have to record a master class for my channel.
Mom: That's fine, honey. Just pick up the phone and cancel.

Me: Mom!

Mom: What?

Me: You know I can't talk on the phone!

Mom: Of course you can.

Me: I can't!

Mom: It's up to you, honey. If you don't want to cancel, that's fine, just go out with him on Saturday.

I give Mom an annoyed look. I really don't like it when she does stuff like this. I remind her that Maureen is *her* friend and if she wants to avoid a disaster-of-unexpected-absence then she'll just have to make that call herself. Then I head up to my studio to finally start my first take.

I know it seems strange for a person with an almost terminal case of social anxiety to have a YouTube channel, but the thing is, it doesn't really feel like Willow is making these videos. I've adopted this persona called 'Kayleigh' and gave her a completely separate personality. Everything I do on my channel is filtered through the Kayleigh persona, and the first few videos were easy enough, anyway. It was just me and my camera. No one knew about my channel. My videos were as insignificant as little needles in a giant stack of needles in a warehouse full of giant stacks of needles.

Pretty darn anonymous.

Then, by the time my first followers appeared, I'd gotten into a routine. It all felt pretty natural. To be honest, I don't even think of my channel as being part of the real world. It's a safe and separate dimension that only exists in bits and bytes.

There's just something very impersonal about sharing your most intimate thoughts on YouTube.

I set my camera to standby and sort my cards. Today's post is about the three-minute-rule. I've been meaning to post about this rule for a while now and I think I've finally gathered enough circumstantial data to stake my claim.

My followers really need to know about this.

YouTube Script:

Obviously you only get one chance at a first impression on that guy you like.

My advice is to never go in unprepared. Don't just try to make up a bunch of stuff on the spot ~~because what'll come out of your mouth will inevitably turn out to be nonsense~~. You should always have a game-plan. You should have something good prepared. Something you've practiced in front of the mirror so you know what it looks like when it comes out of your mouth.

In fact, make a habit of thinking about making first contact with a guy as brain surgery, only slightly more important.

One of the problems you have to overcome with your first impression is the three-minute rule. This rule states that you have exactly three minutes to convince the guy that you're dating material or he'll subconsciously put you in the Bimbo-Zone. And this is not where you want to be. No cool, fun relationship has ever emerged from the Bimbo Zone. It's a bleak, emotionally empty wasteland. And it's almost impossible to get out once you're in.

So this means that you'll have to say or do something quirky and different during those first three minutes. You'll have to make him wake up from his cookie-cutter, PowerPoint world so he'll notice you. And, yes, that means that lines like, 'what do you do,' and 'where are you from' are completely banned from your first conversation.

[Hold up chart 1 [don't smile – it makes you look weird.]]

There are many things you can do to wake him up, but it's probably best to keep it simple on your first try. Just prepare a fun one-liner that he can't respond to on autopilot. Make him really think about what he's going to say next.

[pause for effect]

Don't get me wrong, I'm not talking about cheesy pick-up lines here. Don't go telling him he must've fallen from heaven. Don't say anything even half-way romantic. You don't want to scare him off if he's not into you yet. You just want him to notice you.

Say something funny or shocking ('I heard all guys pee in the shower, is that true?', 'That's a great shirt. Really safe and generic looking, it'd make a great tablecloth.') And make sure you deliver your line with utter confidence. The best joke in the world still sounds flat when it's told by a nervous, fidgety girl, while the worst joke still sounds fine when told with supreme confidence. ~~This is the reason (the only reason!) that confident people seem more sexy.~~

4

The next day drags on like a snail crossing a field of sandpaper and the only time the other temps take a break is when they get together for an impromptu efficiency meeting.

There's no way I can join them, of course, I just don't have the skills to navigate that kind of social interaction, but I do manage to carve out a little time for myself in the afternoon, and use it to get a head start on a new script. That'll save me some aggravation in the evening.

Sadly, my little side project doesn't get close to killing the remainder of the afternoon and, after I've written down every single thing I could possibly want remember about today, it just grinds on like it's my own personal torture chamber. Eventually, though, just when I think time itself may be broken, five o'clock finally does come around.

I grab my coat and head over to the mall.

I really have to make a good impression on SSJ Bailey today. I have to say something halfway intelligent or he's going to think I suffer from some exotic form of brain damage. So I've made a pit stop in the food court to try and fend off another panic attack.

First order of business is getting my breathing under control.

Second order of business is memorizing everything I want to say to SSJ.

Third order of business–

"Hey! You're that girl, aren't you?"

I look up. A tall blond stares down at me, scrutinizing my face. She's fairly pretty, although I can't decide whether it's in spite of, or because of, the fact that her nose is a tad too long and her eyes, ringed and sunken, are oddly colored. In fact, looking closer, I realize that one of her eyes is blue while the other is grey. I'd put her at around twenty-five but for some reason she dresses like she's forty – plaid business suit and way too much foundation.

I'm not sure how to handle this situation. Her presence is making me uncomfortable and it takes me a moment to find my voice. When I do, I tell her I'm probably not who she thinks I am.

"I knew it," she says, sitting down across from me. "You're her!"

Her eyes flit about the food court as if to make sure we're not overheard. "Don't worry," she whispers, "your secret is safe with me."

"I'm sorry, you must have the wrong person," I mumble. "I have to go."

She reaches for my arm and stops me getting up. "I'm Chloe," she says. She digs out a business card and hands it to me. "It's so cool to run into you like this. I mean, I almost didn't recognize you, not with your hair like that and no makeup, but up close, it's unmistakable. You're her!"

"I can't be," I say.

I try to give her business card back but she doesn't take it. Instead, she smiles at me, showing me her teeth. "Do you like them?"

"Your teeth?"

"Yeah. I had them fixed on Tuesday!"

She pauses as if that's supposed to mean something to me.

"*You know*," she prods. "After your video on checking on our tiny flaws in the mirror?"

I Suddenly realize what's going on. Chloe is one of my YouTube followers.

How amazingly unlikely. And how baffling. And how utterly upsetting. I suppose I've always thought of the internet as a kind of separate dimension, my channel as a one-way portal to another world. It's scary to see evidence of my videos affecting actual reality. Chloe must have found me when she was looking for some local channels.

"What about my eyes?" she prods.

Some part of me was wondering about her eyes, yes, but it was reluctant to ask.

"Colored contacts!"

"Ah."

"Yeah, got them two days ago, after your video on having to stand out. You said there had to be something interesting and quirky about us. Something to make us stand out among a sea of seemingly more interesting women. Just so cool guys would remember us, even if we didn't say much."

This is indeed one of my patented insights, but it's one that she's taken way out of context.

"I also have a pink pair," she says. "For weekends."

I mumble she's meddling with the laws of nature.

Chloe beams. "Thanks, Kayleigh!"

I cringe. I suddenly feel like the whole food court is going to gang up on us, tipped off by the mention of my secret YouTube handle. They'll storm our table and tear me to shreds.

Which is nonsense, of course. I don't even have enough followers to fill a tiny bathroom. That's being remodeled.

Still, Chloe appears to spot the panic in my eyes and lowers her voice. "Can I call you Kayleigh? Is that alright?"

"I really wish you wouldn't."

"Okay," she says. "I'll call you by your real name, which is..?"

"You know what," I say. "Just call me Kayleigh."

Chloe smiles and goes on to extract an autograph from me (what can she possibly want with that?) and a fake-smiled selfie (why take a photo with someone you don't actually know?), and then moves in for a long hug (which really catches me off guard).

"I can't wait to see your next video," she says "Could you mention me? That would be really cool."

"In what capacity," I ask, "should I mention you?"

"I don't know." She thinks it over. "As someone you've met?"

I could never do that. I'd feel way too self-conscious dropping names like some kind of, well, popular person. What if my viewers thought I was boasting? Trying to show off? *Look how many people I know! Aren't I cool?* No, they'd see right through me. I'd never live it down. But how to explain this to Chloe?

"Have you watched all my videos, Chloe?"

"Of course! Every single one. Multiple times."

"And do I ever waste your time by mentioning random people I ran into?"

"Actually, no. You're very efficient with our time. It's one of the many things we love about you."

"So," I tell her, surprising even myself, "there's your answer."

Chloe gives me a nod. "Got it," she says. "It was really great meeting you."

She finally lets go of me and, a little frazzled and confused, I walk away. It's finally time to conquer my SSJ Bailey.

Video #76 by *Kayleigh256*. Views: 9

Comments:

ChiqChick: (5:01 pm) YOur such a dork! Just go up to a guy and ask him out if u like him. don't overanalyze everything. and do something about your hair. I know you want to look all cool and mysterious but, damn girl, seriously.

Minnie12: (5:19 pm) Dose nails tho lol!

GettingThereSlowly: (5:19 pm) Great advice, , K. Ur really saving my life here!!

Kayleigh256: (6:27 pm) ChiqChick: You obviously have way too much time on your hands if you can afford to worry about my hair. If you can't think of anything worthwhile to do with your life, here's a tip. There's this thing called grammar. Many of us are using it these days. You should check it out.

ChloeGirl: (9:21 pm) Another great video, K. Will try your suggestions tomorrow on The One!

OldMan1963: (9:24 pm) How are you doing my girl? I can't believe I found you after all these years!

14Donkeys: (9:22 pm) <u>Get premium timeshares at discount prices here!!!!!!!!!</u>

Voedoed: (9:26 pm) Kayleigh is the epitome of what's wrong with the net: too many idiots with webcams calling themselves experts!

OldMan1963: (9:24 pm) Can we get together sometime? I have so many things to tell you, there's so much you need to know.

5

Another little test to see if he's the right guy for you:

Do you like the person you are when you're with him better than the person you are without him?

Somewhat-Square-Jawed Bailey is on duty at the nut store and he smiles at me as I walk in. For all the radiant beauty of his smile, I'm not entirely sure he recognizes me.

"Hello, can I help you?"

I dig down deep for the courage to talk. I find it when I look slightly to the left of Bailey's perfect face. "Sure," I say. "Why not? Now that I'm here anyway…"

His smile warms up. "I meant, what can I get you?"

"I'd like some nuts, actually." I look around the store. "Do you have any?"

I know that wasn't super funny, but that's okay. I'm only breaking the ice here. The good stuff comes later.

Bailey chuckles nevertheless. "You're in luck,' he says. "I think we still have a few lying around. Are you in the market for any particular kind of nut or do you need me to get you one of each? 'Cause that could take a while."

The thing is, there are so many different levels of recognizing someone.

Sometimes you just know you've seen a face before but you can't quite place it. You rack your brain trying to remember where you two met and if you're still on speaking terms.

Other times you remember everything about a person except their name. You spend the whole conversation getting around having to use it…

"I think I'll go for two hundred and fifty grams of peppered Brazil nuts," I tell SSJ, still looking just past his ear.

He nods. "I think we have some in the back. Let me check."

…so I'm pretty sure SSJ Bailey remembers my face. It's unlikely to be entirely new to him. He may even remember that I'm one of his regulars. But that doesn't mean he remembers our last conversation or the fact that it took place yesterday…

"Do you want to make that five hundred grams?" He returns with a big scoop of Brazils, ready to weigh them. "We have a special offer." He points out the flyer on the counter.

… then again, maybe he can't quite place my face.

"Nah," I say, disappointed. "Two hundred and fifty grams will be more than enough."

SSJ rings me up and hands me my change.

I take a deep breath. If I want him to recognize me next time I'll have to rouse him from his PowerPoint world and, if at all possible, make him laugh. (And how cool would that be? Have something that I came up with running around up there, tickling his brain?)

Luckily I know how to make that happen. I know exactly what to say and I've spent a sizable chunk of last night practicing it in the mirror.

Time well spent, if you ask me. An investment in my future. In *our* future. After all, this is going to be the first step towards us starting a life together.

I clear my throat, move my gaze slightly to the right to finally meet Bailey's eyes, and then… well… then my brain totally shuts down. The instant I look into those deep pools of blue, I forget every single thing I wanted to say.

I scream silently inside my head.

"Can I get you anything else?"

This can't happen. Not now! I force myself to say something, anything, and what ends up coming out of my mouth sounds frighteningly similar to, "Crazy weather we've been having lately, don't you think?"

Which makes no sense at all.

Why am I talking about the weather? Especially when it's been particularly homogeneous and completely non-crazy lately?

SSJ stares at me a moment, then nods and says, "You're a bit of a weird duck, aren't you?"

"Sure am," I mumble, feeling my face start to burn. "Thanks for noticing. You're really observant. Anyway, I gotto go."

Without looking up I turn and leave the store.

When I get home there's immediate talk of bedrooms that need to be tidied, trash that should be taken out, turns-of-doing-the-dishes that may or may not have been skipped, pieces of underwear that have been found on the floor (even though we all know ladies never let their unmentionables touch the ground), cartons of milk that have suffered a diminishment of content when no accompanying cups seem to have been used, and, perhaps most important of all, there's mention of a suspicion-of-cookie-theft, specifically from a jar that was clearly labeled 'Mom' for previously misunderstood reasons.

So I spend an hour or so milling around the house trying to put right as many wrongs as I can, then try to make a break for my studio.

"Willow, wait."

Mom corners me on the stairs.

"Everything is fixed, mom, don't worry."

"Do you want me to make that hair appointment for you?"

"What hair appointment?"

"The hair appointment for your hair," Mom says, leaving an excellent opportunity for clarification completely unused.

"I wasn't going to do my hair."

"Really?" Mom looks baffled. "Are you going to meet Maureen's cousin looking like that?"

"Maureen's cousin?"

"You didn't cancel your date, he'll expect to see you tomorrow."

"Mom!"

"What?"

"I'm an adult, you can't just go around making dates for me. I'm pretty sure there's some kind of privacy law against it or something. Either way, I'm not going."

Mom seems confused. "So what you're telling me is that I'm perfectly allowed to cancel your dates, but I can't make them?"

"What I'm saying is that you can, and should, cancel all dates you make for me. And then stop making them. That's, in fact, the most important part. Stop making dates for me."

Mom waves it away. "Well, it's too late now. You can't cancel less than twenty-four hours beforehand."

"It's not a dentist appointment. Of course you can cancel. What's he going to do, charge me anyway?"

"It's just not polite."

"What if I broke my leg? Are you saying that I'd have to hobble there on crutches, just to be polite? What if I died, what then? You really think he'd expect a corpse to show up? Would he go around complaining about how impolite your corpse of a daughter was, just because she didn't cancel twenty-four hours in advance? My thinking here is that sometimes appointments just don't happen. It's part of life. I'm sure he'll survive."

"You don't have to be so morbid," Mom mumbles. "All I need to know is whether you want me to make your hair appointment or not."

"I'd say that would be a 'not', Because I'm not going on a blind date."

I quickly head up the stairs, lock my door behind me, and power up my laptop. I was going to do a quick video on brain freezes – the kind you get when you to try to talk to your crush while looking directly at him – but I suddenly realize I'm not sure what to say about that. I may need to do a bit more research in that area.

And I really can't concentrate, anyway. This blind date thing has thrown me. Just the idea of me going out there and meeting up with some random stranger is enough to give me nightmares.

I look out the window. It's dark already. Somehow I've lost a huge chunk of time. I check my screen but nothing interesting has happened on my laptop. It seems the evening was a waste.

6

I get up pretty early because today's Saturday, backup day. Which means I have a lot to do before my blind-lunch-date.

Backup day may well be the most nerdy, most OCD-type day of the week. It's when I back up all my original video material on an external drive and head over to the post office to put it in a locker. That locker of course contains the results of my previous backup run, another external drive with videos, which I'll bring back home for recycling.

It's not only nerdy to think that my work is backup-worthy, or that something might actually happen to it if I only store it online, it's also pretty nerdy to have not one but *two* external backup drives.

Nevertheless, that's what I do and that's what's happening today.

I know there's probably some mutation of fear at the heart of all this backup making, but, well, sometimes fear makes you prepare for things a little better.

The idea of getting a locker at the post office was a natural progression of that same fear. There's not much point in keeping your backups at home where they can burn down with the rest of your life.

I slide out of bed and start up the backing up process. It runs silently while I dress and brush my teeth.

As always, I remind myself that I really should check my files before I back them up. The data on my laptop could've become corrupted, meaning that I'm now backing up bad data over good data, essentially destroying my work a second time. But, like most Saturdays, I opt to leave it for another time. I'm just not comfortable watching myself. It makes me feel strange, like I'm spying on someone who looks freakishly similar to me. The small amount of editing I do on my videos is difficult enough already, so for now I just make blind copies of my data.

When the backup is complete I take the drive downstairs and have a quick breakfast, then jump into my car.

As I head to the post office, my mind starts to wander. These videos are such a large part of me. On some level they represent the passing of time itself. I sometimes think of my life as a process that simply converts time into videos. Thoughts into pixels. But I know that, eventually, my channel will get lost in torrents of meaningless data. The moment I stop updating (because I'm bored or old or dead) my channel will vanish into obscurity.

YouTube is not an entity to trust your legacy to.

So is it all worth it, then? Should I even bother?

I reach the post office and park in the last available spot. I get out and head inside, my backup drive tucked safely in my backup-backpack. (Where it's wrapped inside a backup-towel, because I lost the original Styrofoam packaging.)

Once inside I take the second drive from my locker, making sure not to bump it against the sides of the metal container, and set it aside. I unwrap the first drive an put it into the locker, then wrap the second drive in the backup-towel and slide it into the backup-backpack.

My data is safe once again.

I leave the post-office and worry again about the value of what I'm doing. The point of creating so much content that will inevitably be lost. Hopefully, there will be two external factors to my efforts.

First, I really believe that I'll eventually crack the seduction code and help Bailey see me for who I really am.

Second, I'm hoping to help others with similar problems.

If I do this right, at least some lives out there will continue along slightly different paths due to my videos.

A pimply-faced kid in Bonaire, for instance, who was convinced her life was over when her friends all started dating, she might just find the courage to come out of her shell. Maybe she'll even grow up to be the first female Prime Minister of Bonaire.

And a forgotten widower in a little apartment in Rome might just find enough bravado to start up a conversation with the woman running the little shop downstairs. He knows not to play it safe because of my videos and he wakes her from her PowerPoint world with an edgy question. Suddenly two lonely lives are melded into one happy one.

And a distraught teen in Greece might watch one of my videos and realize she's not alone. Even if there's no one like her in her little town, or even in her country, there are actually millions of us all around the world. She'll stop thinking about that bad thing she was going to do and try something more positive.

But I'll never know any of this, of course. These stories, if they exist, will never reach me.

I head back to my car and crack a window. It's hot. Should've held out for a spot in the shade. I place the backup-backpack on the passenger seat and strap it in with the seatbelt. I start the car and it suddenly occurs to me that I might actually have followers that I've met in real life. Apart from weird-eyed Chloe, maybe some of the girls who bullied me in high-school found my channel. Or the guys I had crushes on. They could be wondering, right now, why they never realized how special I was.

It's unlikely, of course, highly unlikely, but, well, unlikely is just another way of saying that something is actually possible.

Some of my colleagues could be watching.

Some of Mom's friends.

And maybe, just maybe, my dad…

I leave the parking lot and immediately slam the brakes. Some woman in an oversized SUV cut me off. My right-hand shoots out to catch my backup-backpack (even before the seatbelt brakes kick in), my left-hand offers the woman a very specific finger, and my face communicates clearly that she doesn't need that much metal and plastic to transport her teeny-tiny body to her step-class, but, now that she's basically decided to drive a tank across town, she should probably keep her eyes on the road.

And get off your damn cell! I mouth at her.

She casually shows me one of her own fingers and drives off, all without lowering her cell from her face.

More than a little cranky I slip into traffic behind her and switch on my radio.

Every once in a while that image pops into my head, though, my dad secretly following my channel. Tracking my progress through life from the other end of an anonymous internet connection.

Again, it's unlikely. Very, very unlikely. According to Mom, the man died in a freak accident (one that apparently caused his body, as well as his belongings, and almost every single picture of him, to mysteriously vanish). And I'm not saying I believe that's what happened, but if it isn't, then there's no excuse for him not contacting his only daughter in almost two decades.

Nevertheless, the idea of him checking up on me in some way still spooks through my head from time to time.

I look at my watch: I've got to hurry home if I want to prevent war from breaking out.

Sure enough, Mom's already pacing the living room when I get back.

"Where *were* you?"

"Nowhere," I tell her. "I just had to stop by the post office."

Mom bristles. "You're going to be late for your date." She hands me a stack of clothes. "Put this on, it looks really cute on you." She looks me over for a moment, then her face softens. "Don't worry, okay?" she says. "I know you don't like doing this kind of thing, but he's a really nice guy, I'm sure you two will hit it off. And, who knows, maybe he has a you-pipe-trench too, then you'll have that to talk about."

My brain does a double take. "A *you-pipe* what?"

Mom gives me a look as if I'm slow. "A you-pipe-*trench,*" she says.

I sigh. "Do you mean a YouTube channel?"

"Maybe," she says. "Now hurry, you'll be late."

I change and drag myself to the mall to meet my date – refraining from pointing out the irony of this location to Mom.

Some part of me still believes that this isn't really happening, though. That something will save me.

This could be like the end of act one of my personal movie, where I'm saved from the date-of-doom at the very last second by my Dad. Or by Bailey, who shows up out of nowhere to whisk me away.

Or, you never know, the world might end.

Sometimes you've just got to have faith.

YouTube script:

The majority of our seduction work will take place in something I call 'The Venue.'

This venue is a place where you can run into the guy you're crushing on without looking like a stalker. He's found at the venue with clockwork regularity and you have a good reason for being there yourself. A reason that does not involve him.

[show a graphic with several places crossed out]

The Venue is necessary because our work is done in small steps over a long period of time. Most of us aren't so damn pretty that one look at us locks a guy in forever. And most of us can't show everything we're about in one quick conversation, thus we need to run into him repeatedly.

Moreover, you don't bag a guy who is serious dating material by asking his number in a one-off situation like a club or a bar. His Bimbo-Alarm would go off and any interaction that followed would be a waste of time.

[pause for effect]

So your Venue is probably more like a place of business, a social hangout, or a public area.

And if you don't know what to say the second or third time you run into him at The Venue, just comment on the serendipity of the situation. "Hey, we keep running into each other like this, are you stalking me or something?" ~~Don't forget to smile when you say this!~~

But don't say anything remotely like this if it's clear he doesn't remember you. You don't want him to think you're desperate. In fact, he should never, ever get the impression that you like him more than he likes you. If that thought ever crosses his mind, it's basically over.

[sign off]

<h1 style="text-align:center">7</h1>

I make sure I arrive at the mall a little early so I can swing by the nut store. It wouldn't feel right being here without catching a glimpse of Somewhat-Square-Jawed Bailey. It feels like cheating. Besides, I know what to say to him this time and my stupid brain isn't going to railroad me. SSJ and I are finally going to have a meaningful conversation!

There are a few customers ahead of me but when it's my turn, I definitely see recognition cross SSJ's face.

I guess my 'odd duck'-ness of last time has paid off at least a little.

"What'll it be?" he asks.

I request some of his wonderful peppered Brazils, about two hundred and fifty grams worth.

He nods and disappears to the back. I wait impatiently for him to return. When he does, I get ready to fire off my pre-fab opener. The line to end all lines. The line that I've practiced all evening and that will finally bring us together. But, as Bailey makes eye-contact with me, his pools of blue enveloping me, my brain switches off again. I search for words but all I can find is a large, blank canvas. A pristine sheet of white nothingness. And before I can stop myself, the words, "Crazy weather we've been having lately, don't you think?" come out of my mouth again.

I'm mortified!

My subconscious has betrayed me by over-analyzing that stupid line to the point that it has actually imprinted itself on my brain. It's completely eradicated my wonderful pre-fab opener as the default set of sounds to come out of my mouth.

SSJ Bailey looks at me, a little puzzled.

Emergency sinkhole! Emergency sinkhole!

"You know," he says, after a long, painful pause, "there is this high-pressure front coming in from the west. It should bring more stable weather but recent storms have saturated the air so there might be some unexpected side-effects. Even a small influx of warm air could cause freak storms and hail." He hands me my nuts. "So I suppose that could count as crazy weather, yes."

"Erm, right." I force myself to breathe again. "You seem... erm, very well informed."

"Of course," he says. "You never know when one of your customers will need an in-depth weather report."

"Sure," I say, struggling to find my voice. "That makes perfect sense."

"Or perhaps…" Something mischievous creeps into his voice. "Perhaps I made it all up on the spot."

I force myself to look at him. He's smiling. He doesn't at all look like someone who's busy wondering what kind of idiot I am.

"And, erm, did you?"

"As a matter of fact," he says, "I did. Yes. Come to think of it, it hasn't rained in a while, so apart from being completely fictional, my report was also quite inaccurate."

I smile back. At least I think I do. I can't feel my face. "Very good," I say. "Very clever."

I wish my brain would let me show him how clever I am. Or can be. From time to time. When things line up right.

"Don't sound so surprised," Bailey says. "They don't let just anyone serve nuts, you know. It's very responsible work. You have to have degrees in physics and meteorology, obviously, and ornithology, if at all possible."

"Naturally," I say. "Otherwise it'd be chaos."

"Exactly!"

"So," I say, "you have all of those degrees?"

"Nah." SSJ shrugs. "I only have two. To me all birds look the same, just bags of feathers with beaks."

"That's too bad," I say. "I guess ornithology is out, then."

I realize I say this, not just to keep the conversation going, but also to show him I know what ornithology is. Yup, I'm quite the degree-name dropper if the opportunity arises.

"Oh, yes," he says. "It's definitely out."

SSJ takes my cash and counts out my change. As he gives it to me, there's this strange little moment.

His eyes seem to say; *will there be anything else?*

And then they add; *anything at all?*

And then they add; *like maybe a boyfriend? Because I happen to think that we'd make the perfect couple.*

I smile back, but his gaze starts to drift over my shoulder, and what he really says is, "Who's next?"

I head to the food court a little happy and a little confused.

For all my fumbling I actually think we had a nice conversation. Certainly a step up from our previous conversations. But I didn't get to show him the real Willow (the one he should definitely consider falling in love with), and I'm not sure how much this encounter meant to him.

Maybe he was just joking around like he does with his buddies, killing time at his boring-ass job.

Or maybe he was actually flirting with me.

How am I supposed to tell the difference?

Why don't people communicate more clearly?

We should all prefix everything we say with a little intro. 'I'm going to flirt with you now. Would you like a completely made up weather report?'

'Thank you for taking the time to flirt with me, mind if I stare at my shoes for a bit and try to add to the global temperate by warming it up with my face?'

'I'd expect no less. Now, did you hear about these freak showers we have not been having?'

'I did not, please tell me all about them.'

But no, we just go about our merry subtle ways, assuming everyone around us knows exactly what we're thinking and how our beautiful, bright blue smiles should be interpreted.

It's total insanity.

I arrive at the food court and almost immediately spot my blind-date.

There's only one guy sitting on his own. His back's too straight to look natural, or even halfway comfortable, and he's dressed up as if it's new year's eve. Everyone else here just looks frumpy, disinterested, and is eating with family or friends.

And of course that sneaky little thought crosses my mind: *Why don't you just keep walking? The guy hasn't spotted you yet, you can still go home. Just tell Mom you came down with a sudden case of the plague.*

Except that I really can't.

I'm just not the kind of person who can bail on someone. Even though I really wish I was. Something about these kinds of social situations seems to curb my free will. It turns me into this utterly embarrassed robot that is programmed to do exactly what's expected of her. Even if that something happens to be really uncomfortable, like going on a date with a stranger.

At least it's a daytime date.

In a familiar setting.

So there's that.

This is like a harmless play-date, I tell myself. In fact, we're six years old and about to throw sand at each other.

That image helps me a little, but I still have to use a huge amount of willpower to force myself to go over to his table. And already I feel that weird thing in the pit of my stomach that I always feel when I'm about to talk to someone new.

I take a deep breath, tap him on the shoulder, and say "You must be… my date." Because, well, I suddenly realize I never asked Mom the guy's name.

I hope that doesn't turn into a whole thing.

8

My blind-date looks me over carefully. He's probably wondering why my face is so red and why I'm staring at his ears instead of his eyes – it's that weird thing people do when they meet me for the first time. This guy takes a little longer than most, so he's probably stealing a few extra seconds to wonder why my hair looks that way and why my chest isn't more, well, present. People do that too sometimes, albeit not always so obviously.

"Please have a seat," he says, not getting up from his own.

I pull back the chair opposite him and sit.

"So, your mom said you couldn't wait to go on a date with me."

I cringe and search for a safe place to look. I've seen as much of his ears as any person should have to, so maybe I'll stare at my nails for the next hour or so.

"I'm not sure that sentiment was entirely accurately relayed," I manage to mumble.

He smiles as if he knows what that meant and it wasn't an insult.

As expected, the so-called date starts off rough as the guy, who could be okay looking if he took a little time out of his day to make his eyebrows look a little less like two caterpillars racing to meet in the middle of his forehead, spends a huge amount of time talking about himself. Not just about his boring hobbies (a number of lame sports where he autistically chases different kinds of balls around different kinds of courts with no lasting impact on society), but also about his boring job (some lame thing where he goes to people's houses to switch off their power when they haven't paid their bills), and the boring promotion he thinks he's going to get (some lame thing where he can decide who gets the Saturday shift). And I'd call it all boasting if it didn't sound so much like a bunch of perfectly valid reasons for killing oneself.

Apparently, though, he doesn't see it that way. He keeps on talking and even dons that annoying smirk that guys get when they think they're impressing me.

I really hate when they do that.

It could be my fault, though. Maybe he thinks I'm looking away and turning red because I'm *attracted* to him. It wouldn't necessarily occur to him that I have my own private reasons for turning red and looking at my nails. Reasons that have absolutely nothing to do with him or his arthropodic eyebrows.

Surprisingly, after a while the whole ordeal does become slightly less painful. Bearable, even. Because, for all his chest thumping, at least the guy can talk. I don't need to do much at all. In fact, I think we can get through this entire date with only an occasional head nod from my side. This guy seems perfectly capable of having a date all by himself.

"And get this," he says, "then the guy at the store tells me, 'Sorry Mr. Cooper, but we don't have shirts with sleeves large enough to fit your biceps.' Can you image?" He smiles at me smugly.

I haven't specifically checked out his biceps, but if they were anything special, I'm sure I would have noticed.

"So," he goes on, "I tell myself, don't worry, Bradly, you'll find something cool in the next store, so then I–"

My brain does a double backflip.

Did I hear that right? This guy's name is Bradly Cooper?

Seriously?

Bradly freaking Cooper?

How the hell did that happen? Didn't his parents understand that with the subpar genes floating around inside them the name Bradly Cooper was a definite no-go? Way too hot and manly? I mean, you wouldn't call a fifteen-pound albino baby 'Raoul', would you? Of course not. That wouldn't be right. It wouldn't be fair to the child, who'd grow up to constant looks of disappointment, and it wouldn't be fair to the other 'Raouls', 'Viggos', and 'Brads' out there, who'd surely maintain the correct levels of hard, shredded manliness to support their names.

Bradly Cooper, really?

There should be a law against that.

Or at the least some kind of regulatory body. A group of people who could perform yearly check-ups, make sure that the 'Chads' and 'Brandons' and 'Damons' didn't start confusing all of us.

'Sorry, madam. Your baby simply doesn't have the exotic qualities to become a Paolo. And Titus is also out of the question. He doesn't have Titus legs. See how they point inwards here and here? Those are Wilfred legs if I ever saw any. Or, at a stretch, Harold legs. Tell you what, you work on those legs and come and see us in a couple of years, okay? For now, though, just call the boy Harold. Next!'

I realize Bradly is staring at me.

I've missed a question. (Only his second in more than an hour.) I have no idea what it was so I just say, "Yes?"

"Great," he says. "I think it's important for the girl to have fun on a date, too. Don't you?"

Shoot! Did I just tell him I was having fun?

That really wasn't my goal.

And how gracious of him to think I'm allowed to enjoy myself.

"Guess it was lucky your mom set this up," he says.

"Sure," I mumble, wondering why I continue to lie. Why can't I just be a normal person and tell Bradly that I have to go because I left my cat on the stove? Why can't I come clean and tell him my heart belongs to someone else and that being here makes me feel like I'm doing something terribly wrong?

It's the embarrassed robot, it has to be. It won't let me be openly mean to people.

"So, what do you think?" He moves his chair closer. "Should we, like, make out or something?"

He reaches for my hand and jars me from that safe place inside my head. "You'd like that, wouldn't you?"

I dig deep to find my shaky voice. "Making out?"

"Yeah," he says. "Unless you have an even better idea?"

He smiles knowingly.

I force my brain to get with the program. Now is no time for vagueness and fumbling. For unintentional, red-faced signals. I press on and blurt out, "I'm never making out with you, ever!"

Bradly frowns, a little shocked.

I'm surprised too. I didn't think the social robot would let me be this direct. Maybe it's not such a bad dude after all. Sure, it threw me under the bus a couple of times, but at least it picked me up before the truck came barreling in.

"What on earth makes you think we're at that point in our relationship?" I continue, finding a little more courage.

Bradly stares at me. "What on earth makes you think we're in a relationship?"

And with that statement he pushes me into familiar territory. This is one of my old haunts. This is where I live. In fact, without even thinking about it, I slip into one of Kayleigh's premade, pre-scripted YouTube speeches.

"We're in a relationship," I tell him, "in the same way that every two people on this planet are in a relationship. Relationships are, after all, simply ways in which people relate to each other. For example, my relationship with my dentist is that he checks my teeth twice a year. And my relationship with that woman over there," I point out a mom force-feeding her overweight baby French fries, "is that we've never met. Those are all relationships. All ways of relating to people."

"Is that so," Bradly says. He still doesn't remove that 'you like me more than I like you' expression from his face. "And what, may I ask, is *our* relationship?"

He thinks he has me cornered.

Poor guy.

He can't do battle with Kayleigh. There's no way. She outweighs him by about a thousand pounds of mental prowess and ten thousand hours of over-thinking in this particular area.

"Our relationship," Kayleigh tells him, "is that I was forced to come here by my mom. And that I'm leaving right now. That's all this is."

I can't believe I actually said that.

And I can't believe I'm actually getting up.

In fact, I falter a moment, and right away my mind offers up all kinds of ways I can sit back down and stop people in the food court staring at us. I can apologize and say it was all a joke. I can pretend it never even happened. But I'm relieved to find that I don't. Somehow I manage to push on. I keep walking, away from his table, however unsteadily, however red-of-face and burning-of-ears, and away from the food court.

Yup, I'm getting the hell out of here!

<h1 style="text-align:center">9</h1>

Back in my studio I notice my stack of YouTube cards is threatening to topple off my desk. It's a pretty hefty tower after almost a year of vlogging and I should probably throw the cards out. I never reuse materials anyway, even when I'm explaining similar concepts. Somehow, though, I just can't seem to do it.

If Bailey and I do end up together (which we would, in any sane universe), then these charts serve as a testament to my epic journey. Throwing them out seems somewhat disrespectful.

So I start looking for a more suitable place. I'd keep them under my bed but with Mom's love of rough vacuuming it'd be like storing them in the opening of a particularly aggressive shredder. The bookcases are out too, because I'd have to fold or roll them. The top of the cupboard seems like the only option. If I stack them neatly, and cover them with some newspaper, they should be good for a couple of years.

I hop on a chair and start clearing away the debris that inevitably accumulates on top of cupboards: old stuffed animals, teen idol posters, bits of shiny rock, fridge magnets, pens that are also lights, lights that are also key-chains, and a dusty shoebox that I don't remember putting up there.

Most of the stuff I manage to stuff inside the cupboard, but the shoebox won't fit. I take it over to the bed for further inspection. It looks like it was home to a pair of sneakers at one point, but when I open it up I discover a miniature museum dedicated to my childhood.

On top I find some medals. The kind they give out to kids for attendance of sporting events. Nothing special, but I probably thought they were special at the time. I put them to the side and dig deeper. Underneath I find some magazine cut-outs: houses I wanted to live in, boys I wanted to adore me, places I was going to visit.

I actually remember some of these, but very vaguely.

I put the cuts out to the side as well and dig on. The next layer has an assortment of cereal box prizes – rings with plastic gems, cars and animals, a little magnifying glass.

It feels like I'm on an excavation here, brushing away layer after layer of history, descending deeper into my past.

Next I find a stack of school photos. Each has a little blue circle on it, a magic marker halo around a boy's face. These must've been my childhood crushes. The boys that made me feel happy and sick at the same time. I check the photos with the little magnifying glass, curious if I can still spot the traces of angelic magic I saw as a child.

I never actually talked to any of these boys, of course. I just admired them from afar, waiting patiently for them to inexplicably realize how amazing I (probably) was. I hung around the back of the playground hoping to capture their hearts with meaningful looks that were supposed to convey my hidden depths.

Squinting, I spot Kevin Delany in the first photo. He had the cute overbite and always wore homemade shirts. On the next photo I find Mark, the boy with the scar and the freckles who punched me in the stomach. Then there's Leonard, the boy with the baggy pants and the long hair. He was the only boy to ever invite me to a birthday party. I realize now that he probably invited everyone, but I didn't get that at the time. I followed him around the whole afternoon, waiting for that special moment when he'd take me aside to tell me how cool he thought I was.

Of course, we never actually spoke.

Not at that party, and not after.

I put the photos down. The boys look so different now, alien almost. They've become children when before they were equals. I'm looking at faces frozen in time.

It's difficult not to wonder how different my life would've been if any of these boys had talked to me. Or even looked at me with less than surprise or disdain. If they'd just treated me like a normal girl, no better no worse. But I suppose there was always something slightly off about me.

Then again, would I've developed all the tools I have now? Would I have the insight and the personality to come up with all my videos? A psyche molded under the influence of beautiful memories probably believes, deep down, that the world is a nice place. Filled with wonderful people. And I'm not sure that kind of delusion is helpful. It doesn't exactly prepare you for everything that is going to happen to you.

I check the photos one more time and I think about how much more intense my emotions were back then. How every situation was like life or death back then. There simply were no in-betweens.

I guess it's because your mind needs time to get a handle on emotions. Just like it needs time to learn how to walk, ride bikes, and climb ropes. By the time you reach adulthood you've got it more or less under control; the highs aren't that high anymore, the lows not quite as low. A tuning process has taken place, allowing you to put most things in perspective. The biggest outliers are reserved for situations that really are life or death. Everything else is muted, turned down.

It's true enough that I haven't felt anything as intense as my childhood crushes since. Not, that is, until about a year ago, when I first met SSJ Bailey.

I put the magnifying glass away and move on to the next layer. It contains TV Guide cut-outs of the shows I wanted to live in. Here are the child doctors and child sleuths, the impossibly handsome high school kids, and all manner of people with haircuts that would get them ostracized if they went outside with them today.

The next layer has some bubble gum wrappers and lists of novels.

I dig deeper. Traveling back in time. Getting younger and younger.

More pictures now. These are scratched and yellow, the paper starting to fray from being handled too often. I recognize them instantly.

Picture one: my dad at a hospital, holding a round, purple baby. Of course his hair is way too big and his mustache too thick.

Picture two: my dad and I, eating ice-cream at the beach. I'm about eight, missing some teeth and wearing a wet t-shirt over burnt shoulders. Dad's mustache is gone and his hair has started to thin.

The pictures don't appear to be in any specific order – they were just dumped at the bottom of the box.

Picture three: my dad teaching me to ride a bike. I'm five and my face is a study of terror. I vaguely remember the house in the background, but only from pictures like these, and I can only remember the rooms that were photographed. I have no idea what my bedroom looked like but I recall the living room at Christmas perfectly.

I study my dad's face in the picture. Try to find subtle hints of him thinking about leaving his family. Picking up and vanish. But there's nothing. Nothing to explain why a man who seems so happy to teach his daughter to ride a bike would want to disappear only a year later.

Picture four: A backyard full of people. It's my tenth birthday and the whole extended family has gathered to be photographed. I've always had a special connection with this picture. It affects me every time I look at it, much more than any other pictures of our extended family. Maybe it's because I feel there's something off about this picture. Something I can't quite put my finger on. I look at it a bit longer, wondering why it looks so eerie, why it makes my skin crawl every time I look at it, but I still can't work it out.

Picture five: my mom holding a huge fish, out by a lake somewhere, smiling at the camera. This is an earlier picture than the last one, and mom looks so happy. Much happier than she does these days.

Picture six: a bunch of parents dropping their kids off for a school trip. I can't find my dad anywhere. I check the rest of the pictures but he isn't in them. There isn't even a hole where he might have been.

I blink a couple of times to clear my vision and put everything back into the box. I wonder, ever so briefly, if my dad, wherever he is, knows what still goes through my mind whenever I see an older man in the crowd: *Is that you, dad? Are you secretly checking up on me?*

And I wonder what he'd say about my videos and my PowerPoint Wakeup lines. My little insights into other humans and the strange world around me. Would he be proud of me, of who I've become?

Would he want to know me?

I put the box away. It really doesn't matter. Dad's gone and I don't have time to think about stuff like this.

Video #80 by *Kayleigh256*. **Views: 13**

Comments:

Hopegone72: (8:23 pm) Great vid Kayleigh! Hope I get to try this out on someone cool soon!!!

ChloeGirl: (9:15 pm) Love your premade wakeup-lines, K! I've tried to make up my own but, so far no luck. I don't know how to make them funny or clever :(But I used your Pee-in-Shower line on The One yesterday and it went really well!
We were making small talk and I oculd tell he was running on autopilot (he's in retail). So I decided I had nothing to lose and asked him if it was true that all guys pee in the shower.
First, he gave me this stare, and I started to panic, but then he started to laugh. It was wonderful! Like he opened his eyes and saw me for the first time! Then we started chatting (not just talking, chatting!) I don't even remember what we talked about but whatever it was, it made me very happy :)

14Donkeys: (9:15 pm) <u>Are you too small? Make your member HUGE here!!!!</u>

Kayleigh256: (9:18 pm) ChloeGirl, great to hear the shower line wokrd for you. Yes, you should make up your own wake-up lines, but don't worry, you can use mine till you get the hang of it. So did you ask him out or get his number? You have to keep up the momentum. If you didn't, you will have to force him out of his PowerPoint world again the next time you see him.

ChiqChick: (9:28 pm) Geeks! Your actually proud of talking to a guy? Seriously?

ChloeGirl: (9:28 pm) I didn't, but I'll wake him up again next time. In fact, I'll make sure I don't run into him again until I have something good prepared.

Minnie12: (10:32 pm) This is sooooo sad! How can anyone take advice from this looooser?

OldMan1963: (10:40 pm) Please tell me how I can get a hold of you. I really need to talk to you.

14Donkeys: (10:41 pm) <u>Are you too big? Make your member SMALLER here!!!!</u>

Minnie12: (10:55 pm) I mean, I thought this was one of those ironic channels. These posts are all jokes, right? This Kayleigh person is an actress?

10

A little test to see if He's right for you: *When you talk to another guy, do you keep thinking: this is <u>not</u> him?*

"And?"

Mom stands in my studio doorway. She has a big grin on her face. "How was your date with Bradly?"

"All things considered," I say, blinking against the light streaming in from the hallway, "I think it went rather well."

"Really?" Mom beams. "I told you that you two would hit it off!"

"You sure did. Many times."

I poke a toe out of bed to see if my delicate frame can handle getting up right now.

"So? Did he have a you-pipe-trench?"

"I don't think he did have a you-pipe-trench, Mom."

"Well, it doesn't matter, as long as you had fun. I hope you remembered to make plans to see him again?"

"Even better," I say.

Mom almost explodes with happiness. "Even better?"

"Yes." I pull my toe back in. I should probably stay in bed for at least another hour or two. "We made plans to almost certainly never see each other again."

Mom looks at me a moment, then shakes her head and leaves my room.

I snuggle up against the blankets but suddenly a chilling thought occurs to me. Sure Maureen thought that her cousin was a wonderful guy. But so did Charlie Manson's aunt, before all the trouble. We all assume our family members are probably peachy people. So I might very well have escaped some real harm here.

I toss and turn for about half an hour, but can't find any rest. I decide to jump into my clothes and out of my room. I head for my car and spend the next couple of hours driving. I end up at the park, which is a weird place for me to be.

The last time I was here was probably with my dad. Which tells you how long it's been.

I'm not necessarily an outdoor person, actually. I believe nature is the

44

rightful home of worms and bugs and creepy things. What business do I have in their domain? I mean, ever looked at a tree? I mean really looked at one? Up close? There's like a million tiny things crawling and growing all over it. Tree bark is a moving tapestry of infestation.

Hug a tree? Not my kind of thing.

Still, I have time to kill and nowhere to go so I get out and take a walk. The park turns out to be much smaller than I remember. The spots I loved as a child are still here but they're been crammed together as if space itself has shrunk. The pond where dad tried to teach me to fish now sits directly next to the playground, even though it used to take hours to walk from one to the other. And the field where we played catch is now right across the sandpit.

Walking through the park is like walking through a miniature model of my past. But it's peaceful, at least. No thundering hoovers and complaining moms. In fact, apart from a couple on a blanket near the pond – being way too sickly-sweet together – and a lone cyclist, I'm alone.

I walk on, marveling at the smallness of my childhood-haunts while also keeping an eye on the cyclist. There's something familiar about him. About his build and his movements. And, as he comes closer, I suddenly recognize him. A flood of happy signals washes over my brain and my breath speeds up. I feel like I'm about to run into a minor celebrity.

The cyclist slows and pulls up next to me. He looks me over. "Hey," he says, "aren't you that girl who always buys Brazil nuts?"

Yes! SSJ Bailey recognizes me! And in a completely different context no less!

"Sure am," I say. "That's me. Guilty as charged."

I force myself to keep looking at his face.

"That's weird," he says. "Running into you here."

For a moment I can't respond because I'm lost in his bright, blue eyes. I've always known they were amazing, but I've never seen them in sunlight before. It's something really special. "Uh huh," I manage, "it's very, very weird."

I do my best to think of something interesting to say. At least more interesting than automatically repeating whatever he's just said. Luckily a recent Kayleigh wake-up line actually surfaces.

"Hey." I make a point of looking him over quizzically. "I read somewhere that all guys pee in the shower. Is that true?"

For a second it looks like SSJ Bailey is going to laugh, but then he says, "Do all girls say that? Are you all reading the same blog or something?"

"What?"

"This other girl asked me the exact same thing yesterday."

"Oh."

Damn! One of my fans is using *my* ideas on *my* Bailey! What are the odds? Very low I'd say, for any normal person. In my case, it just shows the universe is indeed out to get me. I've always suspected as much.

Bailey shakes his head, "Girls can be so weird!"

What? No!

I want to shake him and tell him that not all girls are weird, it's just me. I'm the weird one. Or the quirky-cool one. That was *my* line, this other girl's a fake. An imposter. She gets her dating advice from a YouTube channel, how sad is that?

But I can't say any of this. Not without looking desperate and revealing things about myself that are probably worse (like how I'm giving out perfectly good wake-up lines before using them on him – he deserves better than secondhand lines.)

SSJ shakes his head and sticks out his hand. "I'm Bailey, by the way."

I shake his hand and tell him I'm Willow. Meanwhile my brain does a couple of backflips. His name really is Bailey? How's that for serendipity? For fate? For the world giving me a sign that this thing is really meant to be?

Then again, I could've picked up his name in the store subconsciously.

Still. It's a cool name. No one will argue with that.

The perfect name for a long-term boyfriend.

"Well," Bailey says, "it was nice meeting you, Willow."

"Sure, you too."

He's ready to go.

He shouldn't go.

He should forever stay at least at this distance from me.

"Wait!" I say, panicking. "Don't you need a cup of coffee or something?" I immediately feel self-conscious and add, "I have all this time to kill, so I'll probably have to get something."

Bailey thinks this over.

I get busy opening up a sinkhole with my mind. That *should* be possible. Life is all interconnected energy and whatnot...

"Sure," Bailey finally says. "That's not a bad idea."

"Great. There's a nice little café down the road, how about we go there?"

My voice sounds weird. High and nervous and pitchy. Then again, I'm hearing it from inside my head, maybe it's not so bad on the outside. Bailey gives no sign that he's heard anything odd, so maybe I'm okay.

"Cool," he says. "Lead the way."

I do, even though my legs are a bit wobbly, as if they just switched from automatic mode to a mode where they need very detailed instructions on how this walking thing is actually done.

YouTube script:

You've probably heard of the 48 hour rule. It states you can't call a guy until at least two days after your date. But is that really true? And if so, why?

Let's be clear: It's definitely true.
You simply *cannot* call him the next day. Even if he desperately wanted you to call, you still couldn't. If you did, his subconscious wouldn't respect you. ~~It'd send signals to his conscious mind telling him you're a sad loser.~~ And he probably wouldn't even realize this was happening, he'd just feel a little less interested in you when his cell rang prematurely.

~~This is because his subconscious doesn't want to get a call from a girl with too much time on her hands. It wants to NOT get a call from a girl who is way too busy with her exciting life.~~

So how do you get around this? How do you *help* him stay interested? It's simple; you create 'the illusion of scarcity'. This is a trick that's been known in the business world for decades. Anything that looks scarce is instantly more desirable. More valuable. *Only five hundred of these extremely ugly purses were ever made? Great! Quadruple the price!*

We can create our own illusion of scarcity by waiting 48 hours before calling. And this is the minimum amount of time, of course. It's probably best to wait a bit longer. Maybe a full week, or, if you can manage it, a calendar month. ~~But don't overdo it. Leaving it more than, say, a full fiscal year may well be overkill. [note to self: some field testing is needed here].~~

So should we call at all? Shouldn't we just wait to be called?
Maybe. If you're the kind of Barbie doll girl who has cute guys falling over her all day then you could probably sit back and let the world serve you. For the rest of us, for most of us, we might just want to have a little say in what happens in our lives. We might not want to wait around and risk the really good guys getting away while the boring ~~bicep~~ shirt guys hang around. There's no shame in putting effort in going after the things we want.

[sign off]

11

Ever noticed how the fun stuff is always over? How it's never actually happening *right now*?

At this moment, for instance, I should definitely be on a date with SSJ Bailey. I should be sitting across from him, watching him sip his coffee and listening to him talk. I should be looking into his eyes and making him laugh with one of Kayleigh's wake-up lines.

But, for some annoying reason, I'm not. All those moments are gone and I'm sitting on my bed, alone in my studio, thinking too much.

I guess fun moments are always over because we're never fully *in* them. We never pause a great moment to really appreciate it. We just take it for granted. On some level we assume that there are only going to be great moments from here on in. But that's not how it works.

Today, with SSJ, I was definitely preoccupied. I wasn't just worrying about what to say and where to look, I was also highly aware of my stunted outfit and my easily misunderstood body language. And I even found time to worry about my teeth, my hair, my breath, my general height, and whether I was developing a nervous tick in my right eye.

(I wasn't. Turned out to be a one-off spasm.)

The point is, I didn't allow myself to relax and enjoy the moment.

Don't get me wrong; it was all very cool and wonderful and fun, I just wish it wasn't all so *final*.

We should have some kind of technology by now that could record every moment of our lives. Not just the audio and video, we've been doing that for ages, but the whole moment itself, with all its emotions and feelings and physical interactions. We should be able to rewind-and-relive any part of our lives whenever we damn well feel like it. After all, these are *our* moments. We made them happen so we should be able to do with them whatever we want. Live them again. Live them upside down. Back to front. Continuously in a loop. Our moments should be our property forever.

It simply doesn't make sense that each moment only happens once and is then lost forever. That's like buying a movie you can only watch a single time. Where every scene becomes instantly inaccessible the moment you've seen it.

No, this is clearly not how things are supposed to be. We must've messed up somewhere.

Right now, for instance, I want to press my metaphysical rewind button and relive this part of my day:

Bailey looked out across the street at an apartment building as he blew on his coffee. "Wouldn't it be great to own that building?"

It was a stylish, modern affair with tinted windows, higher by several stories than everything around it.

"What if it was yours and you had the money to do with it whatever you liked?"

I felt a glow spread inside me. "You do that too?"

"Of course," he said. "In fact, I've already decided to put a tennis court on the roof, a spa with Jacuzzis on the ground floor, and in the middle I'll install one of those classic 1920s movie theatres."

I nodded. "I can't even get on a plane without sectioning it off in my head. Replace the first five rows with a living room set – couch, big screen TV, media center. Next three rows, a luxury twin bed with slow foam mattresses. Next five rows, a library."

SSJ laughed. "If I ever buy that building," he said, "I'll promise to put in an airstrip." He looked back at me. "What do you say, Willow? Want to land your plane on my building?"

"Of course," I said, because there was no way to aptly express how badly I wanted to land my plane on his building. "We should get right on that."

And there are more moments I need to rewind-and-relive as soon as possible:

I finished my tea and SSJ suddenly reached over and touched my hand. "Don't look now," he said, "but I think that's Melissa McBride over there!" He nodded toward a middle-aged couple drinking tea and looking jaded. I had no idea who Melissa McBride was but I didn't really care. All I cared about was that SSJ Bailey had touched my hand and that he was *still* touching my hand.

"Don't you think she looks exactly like Melissa?"

I stole a careful glance and nodded as if I knew what we were talking about. "Sure," I said. "Spitting image of Melissa. It's amazing, really."

I could only hope this Melissa wasn't an ex-girlfriend. Either way, our hands were still touching.

SSJ smiled conspiratorially. "Should we go over there and ask for a selfie?"

"Maybe," I said. "But I didn't bring my cell. I left the house in kind of a hurry."

"How crazy would it be to ask her for an autograph? Just to see what she'd do?"

"Pretty crazy, would be my guess."

Still touching!

"So, should we go over there?"

"No!" I said, probably a little too loudly. But I couldn't risk Bailey moving even the slightest. Our hands would surely come apart.

"Let's just watch her for a bit," I said. "Who knows what she'll do next?"

And, more importantly, who knows when our hands will (accidentally?) touch again?

"Okay. She could be discussing contracts or something. Do you think that guy is her agent?"

"Could be," I said.

Maybe this Melissa was some actress or reality star. It didn't really matter, all that mattered was that the *'Hey, look over there'* window had passed. SSJ only had to touch my hand for a second to get my attention, everything after that should be considered recreational.

"Or maybe he's her father?" Baily stole another glance. "I mean, beyond a certain age it's difficult to tell, don't you think?"

Still touching.

But what did all this touching actually mean? Did he like me? Did he *like*-like me? Did he… love me?

"I once met this girl who was a dead ringer for Scarlett Johansson," he said, his eyes going distant.

Or did he just forget where he'd left his hand?

"Oh," Bailey said, sounding disappointed. "I think they're leaving."

The couple put some money on the table and disappeared into the street. SSJ pulled his hand back and snapped a quick picture with his cell.

And then there was this moment:

Bailey finished his coffee and smiled over his cup. We had this long moment of eye-contact, the kind where it looked like he might say,

'You're a really cool girl, Willow. We should definitely hang sometime.' Or maybe even, *'You know what, Willow? We should hang every day from now on.'*

To which my reply would be: *'Gee, that's a great idea, Bailey. Why didn't I think of that? Yes, we should totally hang every single day from now on.'*

And then we'd smile a secret, knowing smile because we'd made a pact.

A pact for life.

But what actually happened was that SSJ broke eye contact to check his watch and said, "Got to run. Promised I'd meet up with some people."

Which immediately made me think two heavy thoughts. First, however long I wouldn't see him for, it'd be way too long. Second, why did he say 'people'? Why not just say 'guys?' Was it, perhaps, because these 'people' included girls? Girls who were so hot and modelly that he worried the mere mention of them might obliterate my brittle ego?

It was a distinct possibility.

The best I could do was to show how unaffected I was. (Both by his imminent departure and by his hypothesized meet-up with a bunch of modally models.) So I nodded and said, "No problem. Got a lot of stuff to do myself. In fact, I should've left twenty minutes ago."

"Oh, I'm sorry," SSJ said. "Did I keep you?"

"No!" I blurted out. "I mean, a little, maybe, but it doesn't matter. In fact, it was fun. A lot of fun."

Which had to be the rambling equivalent of shooting yourself in the foot.

"I'll be okay," I said. "How about you? Will you be on time for your… people?"

Bailey shrugged. "Should be okay," he said.

We got up and I followed him to the door. I tried desperately to think of another way to get him to explain who all these people were, but I'd run out of ideas. Out on the curb, he said, "So I'll probably see you in the store?" And with that we parted.

Like I said: everything is always already over.

It wouldn't be so bad, of course, if I could see him tomorrow. If I could just hop over to the store and reboot our conversation. Or if I'd had the presence of mind to tell him, to warn him, that we wouldn't be seeing each other for long time.

12

"Please place your bag on the floor, Miss," the annoyed woman with the impractically long nails says. I wave my right to roll my eyes at her and obediently lift my bag off her conveyor-belt-scale-thingy.

"I can only process one bag at a time," she explains, taping away at her keyboard feverishly.

I shrug and refrain from pointing out that, even though she's doing an impressive job of pretending to be vitally important, we both know, deep in our heart of hearts, that her work is meaningless.

I've checked both of us in online and all that remains is for our bags to be tagged to the right ticket numbers. A computer could do it. And, not to dwell on it, but there are several computers behind us doing that very thing right now. Sadly my travel companion mistrusts the speed and efficiency of computers, which is why I have to interact with Mrs. Nails. But soon, very soon, the manual part of this interaction will be obsolete and Mrs. Nails will sit at home watching the travel channel while consuming her already impressive body weight in potato chips.

In the meantime, I will follow her every order. And I can do this because, unlike her, I'm not motivated solely by the hunger for dominance over others. I just want to get out of here and compliance is clearly the path of least resistance.

"Passports, please," Mrs. Nails snaps.

I dig out my passport and hand it over. "Here you go."

Mrs. Nails taps on her keyboard some more.

"Can I have your bang now, please?"

The first bag slides away into darkness and I lift mine back onto the conveyor-belt-scale-thingy. A little red number shows its weight. It's precisely five kilos under the limit. Which is no coincidence. I expect to buy no less than five kilos of non-essential garbage while I'm on holiday.

It's a tradition.

"Boarding will start in one hour at gate 27a," Mrs. Nails says. "Please be at the gate at least fifteen minutes in advance."

We take our passports and go.

Mom immediately gets sidetracked. "Duty-free!"

"Can't we skip it?"

"Skip duty-free?" Mom looks at me as if I've just suggested using puppies as tennis balls. "Why on earth would we skip duty-free?"

"Because it's a hoax. It's way too expensive."

Mom shakes her head at me. "There's no *duty*, Willow," she says. "It's practically free."

"It's not free. They hike up the price before they take off the duty. Besides, you're just going to buy stuff you wouldn't normally buy, so that's wasted money right there."

"I'll just get some chocolate." Her eye falls on a large chocolate egg, filled with smaller chocolate eggs, filled with cream of chocolate. "Oh, isn't that a great idea?"

"It's not," I groan. "It's a terrible idea. No one needs that much chocolate."

"Don't be silly. It's wonderful."

"I fail to see what's so wonderful about you buying two kilos of overpriced chocolate, which you'll make me carry halfway round the world, after which you'll forget all about it because you never eat chocolate anyway, and me then finding it and eating the whole thing, even though I didn't want to buy chocolate in the first place, just to prevent precisely such a chocolate binge."

"See?" Mom says triumphantly. "You *do* want chocolate."

The thing about this trip is that it was booked way before SSJ and I went for that coffee. Before we'd even made eye-contact for the first time.

I had no way of knowing that when the departure date finally arrived I'd be on the cusp of… well… something.

Mom booked back in January. She said it'd be our last chance to get away before I'd get caught up in my new 'career'. Which seemed unlikely to me, but I warmed to the idea of a holiday because I thought it might give us a chance to reconnect. Or at least connect on a different level from how we were connecting at the time. (Which was very badly and always over something I should or shouldn't do.)

It's the strangest thing, with all her worry about the world, Mom's somehow fine with holidays. The thought of traveling thousands of miles through the air in a metal tube and touching down in a distant land with all new kinds of diseases just doesn't seem to faze her.

Holidays don't appear on her Worry-Spectrum. Apparently she's decided that airlines and tour companies can be trusted to take care of her.

So I was all up for the idea when we booked but, as we got into the taxi this morning, I wanted nothing more than to bail. I wanted to stay behind and work on my strategies. On my scripts. On my wakeup lines. After all, I have to ask SSJ out on another sort-of-kind-of-date before it's too late. Before he forgets all about how much fun we had last time.

It takes slightly longer than forever for the plane to take off.

There are people who can't find their seat.

There are people who can't find overhead storage.

There are people who can't find where they left their baby.

It's always something.

Eventually, though, the plane barrels down the runway and makes that curious jump into thin air. This is the moment I switch off my brain so I can comfortably ignore the fact that the numbers just don't add up. This amount of metal can't possibly leap into the air and stay there. Not at these speeds. This doesn't look close to fast enough.

Mom points out the window excitedly. "Look at the cars," she says. "Look how small they are."

"Yes, they're very small."

"And the houses, see how tiny they're getting?"

"Yes, they're getting very tiny."

"And the river, it looks just like a little snake."

"Yes, the snake is little too."

Mom stops being amazed for a second and looks over at me. "What's wrong? Why are you so grumpy?" She digs out the in-flight magazine so she can check out the airline's newest scams. "We're on holiday, remember?" she says. "You should take a holiday from being grumpy."

And she's right, of course.

I got tangled up in this weird little mood. But she doesn't know. No one knows the dark forces I'm battling. I can actually *feel* the distance stretching out between SSJ Bailey and myself. It's a force as real as gravity and it pulls on me harder the further I move away. SSJ and I are linked by this invisible cord that's reaching some kind of metaphysical breaking point.

I know that for some people 'out of sight' means 'out of mind' but I think for me it's the opposite. With every second that passes I miss him more. And the most annoying thing is that I don't think he misses me. If he did, if he were pining away for me too, this wouldn't be so bad. But SSJ doesn't even know I'm racing away from him. And when I don't turn up at the store today he might start to think all kinds of things. Like maybe I didn't like our sort-of date yesterday.

Which would be terrible.

For all I know he'll go through a miniature Kübler-Ross grief cycle and he'll end up subconsciously accepting my absence and moving on.

I'm in very real danger of losing this wonderful new thing that only just started to maybe, possibly grow between us.

I fidget in my seat and realize I've opened my own in-flight magazine. There's an ad for diamond necklaces, because, presumably, the one thing you really need to buy when you're traveling is fragile, expensive neckwear.

I put the magazine away and sigh. It kills me that I can't contact Bailey. There must be a thousand ways to get a message to him and I don't know any of them. I don't have his email, his cell number, his Facebook page, his LinkedIn profile, hell, I don't even know his last name!

It's too insane to even contemplate. I could tell him every single thing that's going on in my life right now if only I knew the right ten or so characters to do so. It's so incredibly trivial I almost try guessing them.

bailey@miss-u-much.net?

clerkb@nut-stores-golore.com?

ssjforever@hes-like-an-angel.tv?

There should be an app that takes everything you know about a person and then creates a million possible email addresses to which it sends your message. There has to be a market for that.

It makes you wonder how people survived in Victorian times. I mean, think about it. You'd have to write out a letter with a quill, maybe running out of ink and having to go to the store to buy more, then you'd have to bring your letter to the post office in the next town over, riding some type of tall, smelly animal, and wait in line while trying your best not to scream when you realize the last stagecoach left an hour ago and your letter will sit in a sack for the better part of a week before finally starting its nine-day journey to your beloved, who wouldn't be able to get back to you before the end of the next calendar month, assuming neither of the stage coaches got robbed.

No wonder people died so young!

"Anything to drink?"

An air-waitress shoots us a precisely crafted smile from the aisle. Mom orders water with a slice of lemon and I ask for a Coke and orange juice. When the air-waitress takes out two plastic cups, I stop her.

"Just mix them together," I tell her.

The woman hesitates. She's unable to process my request. She gives me two cups, one filled with juice, the other with Coke. Then she quickly moves on to service someone on the other side of the aisle.

"Look," Mom says, pointing excitedly at her in-flight magazine. "They have duty-free nose clippers!"

I take the magazine away from her and get busy sectioning off the plane.

The first five rows will be my studio, so I can shoot and edit YouTube videos even when I'm traveling. The next four rows will be my skylight room. I'll replace a section of the fuselage with a clear material – like a glass-bottom-boat but the other way round – and I'll put a hot tub underneath. The next couple of rows–

"Look! That cloud looks exactly like an apartment building!" Mom points out the window.

The next five rows will be a movie theatre where SSJ and I can watch our favorite–

"Doesn't it look like uncle Dave's apartment building? And that cloud over there, it's the spitting image of uncle Dave himself!" She pats my arm. "Quick, take a picture!"

I wonder if SSJ Bailey ever mixes his Coke with orange juice. And if he doesn't, would he think it's weird or would he think it's endearing? I decide he'd probably think it's endearing.

A cool little image pops into my head: SSJ walking into our home-plane-theatre, carrying a pitcher of Coke-and-orange juice.

Coke mixed with orange juice could be our secret little thing.

Like our song, but with liquids.

13

It's excruciatingly hot. And instead of hiding in an air-conditioned hotel room like, you know, sane people, Mom insists we lounge out by the pool. Presumably so we can get a head start on burning off our skin.

I apply a generous measure of sunblock to my entire body, drape my towel over me, lower my sunhat so it touches my sunglasses, and try to relax.

Subconsciously I scan the pool for competition. Not that I'm competing, of course. I have no interest in any of the fat German men simmering around the pool, not even the younger ones, I just like knowing I'm not the ugliest woman around.

Which, it turns out, I'm not.

Perhaps because it's out of season there's a generous number of older women about, their skin draped sun-blotched and wrinkled around their floppy stomachs, slowly completing their transformations into parchment.

I've always struggled to understand the biological need for skin to get old. There's no point to it. Or maybe there is. Maybe it's some kind of evolutionary deterrent.

You have achieved your biological purpose. You are no longer required to reproduce, so now you get to look like dried fruit until you die.

Something bright and languid enters my peripheral vision. I lift my sunhat so I can move my head, and spot the source of the brightness.

It's one of *them*.

Of course it is. There's always at least one.

Wherever you go, whatever time of year, there's always at least one stupid chick with perfect skin and a perfect figure rocking a perfectly small, white bikini.

Always.

And, like always, I instantly dislike her.

"Can we go inside now?"

"Willow!" Mom says. "We just got here."

"We got here over an hour ago. And I'm pretty sure we're not even supposed to be outside between twelve and three, with the ozone layer disappearing and everything."

Mom shakes her head as if I've suggested killing baby pandas for sport. "Let's not waste our first day of sun."

"We're not going to run out of sun any time soon." I take off my towel and get up. "I think I'll try to find some shade."

"Be a dear and do my back first?"

I take out our tube of SPF 100 and start grinding it into her skin. This stuff is like rubber cement.

Mom's a bit like an accountant when it comes to holiday sun. Sometimes I think she mentally divides the cost of the holiday by the number of sun-hours she gets, arriving at the cost per hour. The more sun-hours to divide by, the lower the cost per hour. In fact, burn off enough skin and your holiday is practically free.

"Don't forget the back of my arms."

"I'll double layer them, don't worry."

As I cement away, I wonder about SSJ Bailey's holidays. Does he travel abroad? Does he tan or burn? Does he get drunk and sleep around or does he maybe, just maybe, go on holiday with his mom and think about me?

"I'll have one of those with the little umbrellas."

"You want a Piña Colada?"

"Is that the dark one with all the chocolate? Because I don't like chocolate."

"What do you mean, you don't like chocolate? You made me carry kilos of the stuff on the plane!"

"No," Mom says, "you know I don't like chocolate in my drinks."

The hotel entertainment has just started. It's some kind of dancing, singing, magic type show they assume tourists like. Two colorfully dressed members of staff dance around on stage urging the guests to join in.

Mom found a table right at the front so she wouldn't miss a thing. The other tables are filling up as people return from their after-dinner strolls.

"Piña Colada isn't chocolate," I tell Mom. "It's coconut."

"Okay," she says, relieved. "Because I just *love* coconut."

"No you don't. You never let me order Indonesian takeout because they use too much coconut."

"I mean, I love coconut when I'm on holiday."

I shrug and head to the bar. I get Mom a Piña Colada and select something suitably strong and colorful for myself. When I return, Mom looks disappointed.

"Oh," she says, "Thanks. That looks… good."

"What's wrong?"

"Nothing's wrong, Willow. I'm sure this drink will be fine."

"Something is wrong, just tell me."

"It's not important."

"You asked for a Piña Colada. This is a Piña Colada."

"No," she says. "*You* said I wanted a pina-lada, I asked for a drink with little umbrellas. This drink has exactly no little umbrellas. But that's fine, you just sit and enjoy yourself."

"I'll get you some little umbrellas."

"Never mind. This drink is apparently not supposed to have little umbrellas, adding them now isn't going to change the taste."

I sigh and drop into my chair. I really don't have time for all this umbrella drama, something Bailey said has suddenly started gnawing on my brain.

He'd already heard my PowerPoint Wake-up line. The one about guys peeing in the shower. Did he overhear it somewhere or was it used directly on him? And, if it was, what happened after? Did this thieving girl become Visible to him? And did he realize she was flirting? Did he maybe even *like* it?

Whatever the case, it appears I have a rival.

An adversary. An arch nemesis.

"Stop fidgeting," Mom says. She points at my leg which is bouncing up and down for no reason.

I've also started biting my nails.

"I'm getting another drink, you want anything?"

Mom gives me a meaningful look.

"Umbrellas, got it."

The next couple of days go by fast. We spend a lot of time eating, shopping, and napping. On the fourth day we discover an authentic little restaurant a few blocks from our hotel and from then on we end up there most evenings. The ambiance is relaxed and the owners, an elderly couple deep in their seventies and still clearly in love, are the friendliest people you could ever hope to meet.

One evening, as we order mixed seafood drenched in garlic, I look over at Mom and notice she almost looks like she's enjoying herself. Her head moves to the whispered music of the old couple's radio and a new, serene kind of smile forms on her lips.

I can't help but watch her. It's like witnessing a miniature transformation. The hard lines on her face lose their definition and her brow slowly slips out of its permanent-worry position.

It makes me think of the carefree mom my aunt told me about. The one who wasn't always scared of everything.

"How do you feel, Mom?"

She doesn't answer, not right away. Her eyes are distant as she nods to the music. I start to wonder if she's even heard me when she finally answers. "You know, Willow, this reminds me of summer holidays with your grandparents."

"It does? Where did you go?"

"Oh, we didn't go anywhere. We stayed in our backyard. But we'd put down this huge, colorful picnic blanket and sit out all evening drinking home-made lemonade. It was so peaceful..."

Her voice trails off and I keep watching, fascinated. Maybe this is my chance to have a real talk with her. To have some kind of interaction that's not based on making plans or fixing problems.

"What did that feel like?"

Mom puts down her fork and takes a moment to order her thoughts. When she speaks again her voice has a soft, singsong quality to it. "It was just such a lovely atmosphere," she says. "A cool breeze after a hot day. The whole family together. Mom and Dad telling stories.

"I was out of school for the summer and it felt like a whole new world was opening up. Endless days of fun and freedom."

"I used to have the same thing," I tell her. "When I was little the holidays always seemed endless. I can remember how shocked I was when I figured out it was actually only six weeks. To my child brain it always felt like months."

Mom gives me a sad little smile. "And you had such a hard time going back to school."

"I did, but not because of school. I don't think I really minded school itself, it was just that there were so many people."

"I never understood that," Mom says. "I always loved seeing my friends again after a long holiday. But you thought going back to school was the end of the world."

I finish my wine and signal the old lady for a refill.

"It was, in a way. I had to move out of my safe little world at home, where I could read and think and play, and go back into the cold, noisy chaotic world of middle school. It was really jarring."

Mom reaches over and squeezes my hand. "You don't know this," she says, "but it was always very hard for me to drive you back to school."

"That's not how I remember it." I think back and smile. "You were like this middle school-Nazi, unflinchingly following orders. You didn't care how much I begged or pleaded."

"On the outside, maybe, but on the inside I wanted nothing more than to turn the car around and drive my little girl back home."

The old lady comes over and pours us more wine. We sit in silence for a while, sipping away and enjoying the atmosphere.

I feel a little glow inside me.

I can't believe how well this is going.

I can't believe Mom is finally opening up. We haven't talked like this in years. She's always so guarded, so careful. Weighing every word and ending up talking about nothing but rules and warnings.

The music changes to something slow. I decide it might be safe to try a more daring topic.

"So," I say, keeping my voice soft. "I was always curious. Before I was born, did you and Dad ever go abroad?"

Mom doesn't answer. I look over and see that same distant look still in her eyes, but her head has stopped moving to the music and some of the lines in her face have returned.

"Mom?"

"You know what," she says, "I'm pretty tired. I think we should turn in."

And with that the evening is over.

YouTube script:

It's important to remember that you can approach a guy whenever you want, in any given circumstance, whatever's going on. You don't have to wait for what you think will be the perfect opportunity.

Although women definitely have to be in the right mood, in the right frame of mind, to deal with some random guy wanting her number, guys don't work that way.

It doesn't matter what they're doing, they could be on their way to hospital with a broken leg, a punctured lung, and one eye poked out, and they'd still notice a cute girl. In fact, a beautiful enough woman could probably break into their home and wake them from a deep sleep just to say 'Hi, what's your favorite color today?' and they'd be fine with it.

But that doesn't mean it'll be easy. It doesn't mean you don't have to come prepared. An average looking woman (and that's most of us, face it, that's what *average* means after all) will remain mostly invisible to a cool guy. ~~There will always be white bikini chicks to lightening rod his attention away from you.~~ And you'll remain invisible right up to the moment you wake him from his PowerPoint slumber with a weirdly cool action or comment.

Granted, they won't exactly bump into us or knock us over, ~~that'll only happen to some of us some of the time~~ but before you wake him up you'll register as brightly on his mental radar as a lamppost or a mailbox. Action is required.

So no more excuses! Prepare some cool lines and get out there and practice!

[sign off]

14

We're not that different from the quantum particles we're made of: we don't feel we truly exist until someone observes us.

The office is deathly silent as Gary makes his rounds. Meanwhile, I'm staring at my screen, amazed at how fast that holiday feeling disappears. It's as if the surface of my desk is a superconductor for holiday feelings. The moment I touched it, all those bright happy thoughts got sucked right out of me. Even rubber gloves wouldn't have helped. Touch that surface for a second and you're definitely back in the real world, feeling as if you've never been on a single holiday in your entire life.

In fact, I'm already in need of another break.

On top of that, I really wanted to go by the nut store before work to see Bailey, but the jetlag messed me up and I overslept. Dropping by the store would've meant taking a half-day and I didn't want to do that. I'm saving my days. I won't touch them till SSJ and I are an item and we can touch them together.

Spend them together, I mean.

Anyway, it kills me that I haven't seen him in such a long time. (Only slightly shorter than forever.)

"What's going on?"

Gary steps into my cubicle. He taps my desk and he gives me an odd look. I immediately start to panic. "I'm sorry?"

"You're way behind on your reports. Some of them were due last week."

I struggle to follow his defective reasoning. "This is my first day back. I was on holiday last week."

"On holiday?" Gary frowns. "Are you sure?"

"Pretty sure, yes."

"Didn't we talk about the Mundial report on Friday?"

"I don't think so," I stammer.

"Then who did I talk to about that?"

"I really wouldn't know. Because I wasn't here. I was on holiday."

"Didn't I see you getting a coffee?"

I shake my head. "You didn't. I don't drink coffee, and also I wasn't in the country."

Gary gives me a look as if I might still come around and realize I'm mistaken. When I don't, he continues. "You know you have to tell Beth when you're leaving, don't you? She needs to put it in the system."

"I did," I mumble, but Gary's already left.

When my lunch break comes round I drop everything and hurry to the mall. As I get close to the nut store, I suddenly start to feel unwell. Out of nowhere I'm all sweaty and nervous and panicky. I don't understand why because I didn't eat anything weird for breakfast.

I manage to drag myself into the store, though, and get in line. When it's my turn SSJ Bailey smiles and says, "Hey, there. What'll it be?"

And, even though I'm insanely happy to see him, my upset stomach curbs my enthusiasm. I only manage a barely audible, "Oh, just my usual."

Bailey's smile wavers. "Your usual? What's that?"

This isn't good.

My voice cracks. "You know," I prod. "I'll have a hundred and fifty grams of the nuts I always get."

Please remember me!

"Hold on." SSJ looks over at the other clerk, a new girl with a long nose and earrings in odd places. "Did you order with Teresa, maybe?"

At the mention of her name, Teresa looks at me. She shrugs and turns back to her own customer.

"I'm sorry," Bailey says. "Ter. doesn't seem to remember you. Did you order ahead?" He goes over to the ancient computer on the counter and taps away on it. "Maybe I can find you in here."

"Never mind," I mumble. "I'll just have some of your peppered Brazils."

I really wish I hadn't come.

I really wish I wasn't even on this stupid planet.

By now I feel so ill that I consider looking for a medical professional before I collapse.

SSJ returns with my Brazils and rings me up. "So," he says, "I guess you'll want something to go with that order?"

I'm not sure what he's talking about, I must have missed something subtle in our interaction. That's not surprising, apart from being a social dimwit, I also appear to be dying at the moment.

"Don't you need an up-to-date, completely factual weather report?"

Bailey grins at me mischievously.

It takes me a moment to realize what's happening, then another to recover from the shock.

SSJ does *remember me!*

"Because," he says, "there's all sorts of meteorological stuff going on right now. High and low-pressure fronts are bursting in from all directions. It's like an epic weather battle, right over our heads. Marvel Studios is going to do a whole series of bad movies about it."

"Oh, don't worry," I say, getting into form. "I don't need any more weather reports. I have a sizable collection already. I was actually thinking of auctioning them off to the highest bidder."

"You were?" Bailey seems curious where I'll go with this.

As am I.

If only I knew.

"Sure," I say. "Some of the reports in my collection are, erm, really old. Antiques even. I should be able to get a pretty good price for them on one of those reality shows where they pawn stuff. Although I might need to learn to haggle, because that's not part of my natural skill set."

"Wait a minute!" Bailey says. "I copyrighted some of those reports, you know. You'll have to give me a cut of the profits."

"Naturally. You could put it towards that building you liked so much."

Bailey smiles. "Oh, yeah. I almost forgot about that."

There's a long pause that's made up almost entirely of eye-contact.

Sweet, light-blue eye-contact.

"We should work out the details over another coffee, don't you think?"

He nods enthusiastically. "We definitely should."

I'm not sure if he still thinks we're joking.

Because I'm not.

Not even a little.

"How about this afternoon? I could come back around five?"

Which should give me enough time to find out what kind of disease is currently tearing away at the lining of my stomach. Yup, I should definitely be out of hospital by then.

"Oh…" Bailey's smile wavers. "I don't think I can. Sorry. There's something I have to do this afternoon."

That was a pretty clear signal. No doubt about it.

My stomach does another cartwheel and I realize it's probably for the best that Bailey doesn't want to meet up. I could be in hospital for a long time.

"No problem," I manage. "It was a stupid idea anyway."

I turn to go but Bailey calls me back.

"Hold up, Willow," he says. "What about tomorrow?"

I shrug. "I'd have to check my schedule."

When I reach my car I realize my stomach is doing much, much better. Whatever was attacking me must have given up.

Video #84 by *Kayleigh256*. **Views: 9**

Comments:

ChloeGirl: (6:12 pm) U were right about being invisible until you wake a guy up!! I was on a date with my cool new guy and I asked him about all the times we spoke before we started dating. you know, what he thought of me and why he never made a move, and, as you predicted, he didn't even remember seeing me before! Very, very humbling… All those times we made eye-contact (extended eye-contact!), all the times we spoke (9 times!), that time we shared an elevator (exceptionally special!), he couldn't remember any of it! It's like it never even happened. The only person on the planet who knows that even happened is me :(

Kayleigh256: (7:27 pm) Don't let this drive you crazy. Keep it in perspective. Just because he doesn't remember some moment that was special to you, that doesn't mean you guys aren't right for each other. But this is a good reminder that you should always have something cool or funny or cute prepared when talking to your crush. Unless you wake him up from his PowerPoint world, you'll stay part of the background noise of his life.

Minnie12: (7:37 pm) All your advice, Kay, makes so much sense, I can't believe I didn't figure it out before!

ChiqChick: (7:37 pm) Seriously, my ovaries hurt when I read this crap! Over-analyze much?? Extended eye contact – what the hell is that suposed too be? Just check if the dude has a nice watch and clean shoes, that means he's got money, and if his face doesn't make you feel all dry and shriveled then take him home. I should set up my own channel, teach you losers how the real world works.

OldMan1963: (8:27 pm) NOt everything your mother has told you is true. Can we meet sometime?

Hopegone72: (8:27 pm) So go do that, CHiqChick. Set up your own bimbo channel and stay off this one. No one here is the least bit interested in what you have to say!

ChiqChick: (8:39 pm) 'the least bit interested'?? Who talks like that? I don't understand a thing ur saying!!

Hopegone72: (8:40 pm) Which is exactly my point.

OldMan1963: (8:44 pm) Please let me know how I can reach you Willow.

15

Mom's on the phone when I get home. I kick off my shoes, give her a kiss, and get ready to head upstairs. I desperately need to prepare for my this-is-almost-certainly-a-date thing of tomorrow. But Mom holds me back at the last second and presses the receiver into my hand.

"Someone wants a quick word with you."

"Mom!" I hiss. "I can't talk on the phone!"

"It's just Brad," she says. "It won't take a minute."

"Brad? What Brad?" I try to hand the receiver back but Mom won't take it. She jumps out of reach of the ancient cord on our ancient landline. Mom can be surprisingly agile when she wants to be, and she's not above exploiting my social robot flaw. She knows I can't just drop the receiver.

"Just say a quick hello," she says sweetly.

The robot raises the receiver to my ear. "Hello?" it says, "This is Willow?"

"Hey! Brad here. Just wanted to say I had a great time last Saturday."

"Oh." I still have no idea who this is or why I should be updated on his Saturdays. But he does sound a bit hot. A bit handsome and square-jawed. I can almost picture some cool guy on the other end of the line, smiling at me all square-jawed. Which doesn't exactly help in the being-able-to-talk-on-the-phone department.

"Think we should do it again?" he says. "Maybe we can catch a movie tomorrow?"

My beautiful fantasy shatters and I shoot a look at Mom. I recognize the voice now, and it's not some mysterious, hot guy. Some cool, SSJ-ed man wanting to sweep me off my feet. This is just Bradly Cooper, the Caterpillar Eyebrow Guy. And I already did my bit for humanity. It's some other girl's turn to take him out. This should be like jury duty.

"I'm pretty busy," I tell him. "I have this channel and I have to make updates and stuff. Bye."

I hang up before he can talk over me.

"Why did you do that?" Mom gives me a look as if I've just killed all her future grandchildren.

"I can't see him, okay? I'm busy."

"You're not busy. You're just hiding in your room, making videos for five other girls hiding in their rooms."

"It's more like thirteen," I say. "Thirteen *women*. And we're not hiding, we're doing valuable social research."

"Give me one real reason or I'm calling Maureen and making the date myself."

"Mom!"

"I mean it!"

We stare at each other. A Mexican stand-off. (At least, I think it's a Mexican standoff. Maybe that takes three people. Either way, Mom and I are more or less stuck.)

"Look," I say at last, "I really can't go, okay? I have this... thing."

Mom looks at me dubiously.

"I do! I'm meeting up with this guy from the nut store. His name is Bailey and he's really funny and smart and, well, everything that Bradly is not."

Mom suddenly melts. "Bailey, huh?" she smiles. "Okay, we'll see how that goes."

I'm confused. I thought she was fully on Team Bradly Cooper, ready to fight tooth and nail for her future caterpillar grandchildren.

"You're not mad?"

"Of course not," she says. She ushers me up the stairs and follows close behind. "Tell me more about this Bailey. How tall is he?"

"Pretty tall, I guess."

"Good. That's very good."

I head to my studio, still somewhat stunned. I guess as long as there are possible grandchildren in the future, Mom's okay. "Show me what you'll be wearing," she says, following me in.

I shrug, I haven't really thought about it. I open my closet and take out a clean pair of jeans and my favorite t-shirt.

Mom sucks air in through her teeth. "Are you sure you want to wear *that*?"

"What's wrong with it?"

"Nothing, if you want him to think you're his new best buddy."

She rummages around in my closet and she's made me just about insecure enough that I don't mind.

"You dress like a homeless person," she mumbles.

"Mom!"

"On crack."

She takes out a couple of old dresses – which she bought for me and I never wore – and lays them out on my bed. She still doesn't look happy.

"Is there any chance you'd let me take you shopping?"

"I can't go anywhere tonight. I need all the time I can find to prepare my opening statements for tomorrow."

"Opening statements..." Mom gives me a look but lets it go. She picks out a black dress with way too many lacy bits and stands me in front of the mirror. "How about this?"

I know how this looks, but my mom's not dressing me. I just have a private wardrobe consultant who happens to be related to me.

"It's a bit ... old fashioned, isn't it?"

Mom shrugs. "You're the one who doesn't want to go shopping. Anyway, this is much better than that t-shirt. At least it shows you're female."

I stare at myself in the mirror and I just don't know anymore. Is this better?

I barely make it to work on time the next morning. Gary's already on his rounds so I have to slip into my cubicle stealthily, which isn't easy in a dress. Or maybe it's just my imagination that I stand out like a deep sea buoy in a desert.

I feel like an exaggerated version of myself. Like one of those Pop! dolls with the big heads. 'Pop Unknowns: Willow in Almost-date Dress – limited edition.'

I turn on my computer and hear Gary somewhere in the distance, telling one of the new guys about his strict closed-door policy. I hope the guy realizes that Gary isn't joking. He wouldn't be the first to make that mistake.

With my head down I handle a couple of reports, then leave the building at precisely twelve to arrive at the nut shop just as Somewhat Square Jawed Bailey steps out.

This is very upsetting. I specifically came early so I'd have time to center myself and practice my opening lines. Instead I find myself staring at SSJ with kept breath and a little star-struck. (Again I feel as if I'm meeting a minor celebrity. It's very annoying.)

"Hi!" he says. "I thought I was a bit early, but you're here."

I nod. There's probably a really cool response to that but I'd have to go home and think it over for a couple of hours to find it. Instead, I just say, "Hi yourself."

"So," he says, looking around. "Where should we go? I only have forty minutes."

I'm back on familiar ground. I have our whole lunch planned out. I know SSJ doesn't have much time. I also know it's too early in our not-yet-relationship to go anywhere by car. And I know I could scare him off if I make too big a deal out of this. So, taking this and much, much more into account, I've come up with the perfect spot.

"There's this cool little jazz café just outside the mall." Or so Google Maps told me last night. "Want to go check it out?"

SSJ smiles. "Sure, lead the way."

<h1 style="text-align:center">16</h1>

As we make our way to the escalators I'm acutely aware of walking next to SSJ Bailey. Of him walking next to me. Of us walking together, next to each other, like real people.

I know we're just going for a sandwich and it probably means nothing to him – not enough at least to cancel whatever he was doing yesterday – but I still catch myself thinking: People watching us probably assume we're together. And that's a fun little thought. So much fun, in fact, that I take a few moments to imagine what it'd be like if SSJ and I were a real, official couple.

For one thing, I wouldn't have to wait ages to see him again. We'd just meet up again after work. We'd go home and make dinner, fight over the TV remote, and snuggle up to a good movie.

And it would be great. In fact, even having a fight with him would be wonderful. That may sound insane, but a fight would make this whole thing real. Fighting is a sign of investment, after all. You don't fight with someone you don't care about. You just walk away.

"So," he says, "how did you find this jazz café thing?"

"Oh, it's just one of those cool little places where I like to hang out."

Just a tiny lie to make me look more, well, human.

"Great. Show me the way."

SSJ Bailey sounds a bit nasal today. I think he might be coming down with something. I watch as he touches his nose and realize that being ill really suits him. It makes me want to take him home and wrap him in blankets and feed him oodles of placebo-effect inducing soup.

"By the way," he says. "That's a really nice dress."

I look over at him to check if he's still talking to me.

He is.

"It looks good on you."

I shrug because it's the only response I'm capable of. As he looks me over, I feel all warm and fuzzy. I make a mental note to find more ways to get him to look at me like that.

"You look good too," I finally manage.

Bailey snorts as if I'm joking. Which makes him even more adorable. I look away before I get too nervous to talk to him.

"So," he says, "do you have a funeral later?"

"What?"

He shrugs. "I'm just saying, not many people actually look good in a funeral dress, so you shouldn't feel embarrassed or anything."

"Oh," I say, a little befuddled. "Thank you. Yeah, I just don't have time to change later. I hope you don't mind?"

He waves it away. "Don't worry," he says. "Was it someone close?"

I struggle to keep the lie going. "No, just a step-aunt. Twice removed. So, you know, I'm not super sad or anything."

"Good." He gives me an encouraging smile.

We exit the mall and I lead us across the road. I do my best to remember the route while simultaneously looking as if I know where I'm going. Our arms accidentally touch and right away I stop caring about the route or my walk or my dress.

I don't pull away, and Bailey doesn't either. Our arms stay silently connected as we walk. I hold my breath to enjoy the sensation more.

Is this an accident? Does he know this is happening?

I want this to last for at least forever so I remind myself to breathe again, just in case it does. When we reach the café I feel a pang of loss as we go inside and our arms disconnect, but the loss it doesn't last long. Bailey finds us a table and, before I know it, I'm sitting across from him looking deep into his amazing eyes.

My first thought is that it should be illegal to have such amazing eyes. I mean, hundreds of girls will see these eyes and daydream about them, but only one of us gets to take them home. For the rest of us they're just more torture to be added to our day.

Yup, this should definitely be illegal, for anyone but Bailey.

"It's a really nice place," he says, looking around. "I'm glad you didn't suggest some kind of dopey, romantic place."

"Well," I say, "this place is somewhat romantic, isn't it?"

Bailey laughs as if I'm joking. He leans over and squeezes my hand and I decide that I probably was joking.

"You're right," he says. "I just remembered that Jazz Café Monthly voted this place the most romantic spot in the city, three years running. Then again, they might be a bit biased."

I smile. He sounds so cute making jokes in between sniffles. I just want to hug him and kiss him and blow his nose for him.

I have no idea what that means.

"So," he says, "if you can forgive how cliché this will sound, I actually have a question for you."

"Shoot."

Do you realize how perfect we are for each other?

Does it really make sense for us not to be a couple?

"I was genuinely wondering if you come here often." He smiles sheepishly. "I mean, because you recommended it."

"Not really," I say.

If life were more optimal I'd come here at least three times a week with a bunch of really cool, interesting friends. Sadly, a social curse placed on me at birth prevents life from being more optimal.

"How about you?"

He gives me a look. "Do *I* come here often?" He shakes his head, smiling. "No. Then again, given the fact that I just found out about this place two minutes ago, I'd say that's not too surprising."

I feel my face burn. "I mean, do you come to places *like* this often?"

But what I really mean is, *do you date a lot? Do you have a girlfriend? Do you maybe have a girlfriend and a wife and an admirer and a bunch of baby-mommas? Just asking.*

But, annoyingly, SSJ just shrugs.

Which gives me exactly no information.

And that's my least favorite amount of information.

Our almost-certainly-a-date lunch is of course over far too soon and, before I know it, we're heading back to the nut store.

I feel a little overwhelmed. Again I spent way too much time thinking about what I should say and do to actually enjoy myself. On the upside, I don't think I made any big mistakes, and Bailey didn't run away screaming, so I'd say: mission accomplished.

I'll find some time to relax and enjoy myself when we're married and our third child is on the way.

We get to the store and there's this awkward moment where it feels like I'm dropping him off. For a second or so I even wonder if we're supposed to kiss. (Do people kiss goodbye at the mall? Is that accepted behavior? I really don't know.)

We stand for a moment, silently. Two women in way-too-tight leggings walk by.

"So," Bailey says, "That was fun, right?"

"Yeah," I say, "You're really good at, erm, lunch."

I cringe. My preparations didn't include closing statements. Classic rookie mistake. Won't happen again.

I'm about to give it a second try when my train of thought completely derails – SSJ is sliding his hand down my arm! I have no idea what to do, and SSJ's expression doesn't tell me anything. He just smiles this usual, casual smile. When his hand reaches mine, he takes my cell and says, "Here, I'll give you my number. Just in case we need to message each other."

He types in his digits, hands me back my cell, and disappears into the store.

It takes me a moment to realize I'm supposed to go away.

Back to work or something. Back to the real world.

YouTube Script:

So here's my take on beautiful people. On the white bikini rockers by the pool, the hair-flipping waitresses at the jazz café's, the push-up-bra-and-leggings babes swarming the mall.

I feel sorry for them.
Here's why.

In many ways life is like a prolonged session of Russian roulette. It's a dangerous game of chance that can leave you hurt at every turn. First, millions of sperm-cells (millions of possible Yous!) race along the fallopian tubes, but only the winner gets to enter the egg. The rest of the Yous just die. If you're the one who made it, then you're literally one in a million. Sadly, this just means your struggle is about to begin.

Next spin of the barrel: will you get good parents or bad?
Next spin of the barrel: will you be born in a nice part of the world or no?
Next spin of the barrel: will you get any hereditary deceases or not so much?

Let's assume you lucked out again: good parents, pretty nice part of the world, no diseases. Well done!

But now you pick up a mirror. Next spin of the barrel: are you ugly or beautiful? Chances are you already know. If you happen to be beautiful your extended family has told you this hundreds of times (can't trust your parents). And if you're ugly, or different in any way, then your little pals at school have found some pretty efficient ways of notifying you.

Still not sure? That just means you're one of the beautiful people. You don't know any better. You may even have some silly questions like:

Doesn't everybody have boyfriends all through high school?
Doesn't everybody have people fall all over themselves trying to help you out?
Actually, they don't.

Doesn't everybody get their dream job when they smile at an interview? Isn't that how the world works?
It most certainly is not.
That's just how things seem *to work inside the temporary Beautibubble.*

But, as I said, we should feel sorry for these people. They're not the lucky ones here. They didn't actually draw the longest straw.
Think about it. You don't learn much when you just breeze through life on the kindness of others. When you grow up thinking the world is filled with smiling, friendly people just waiting to help you.
The way you learn is by having to fight every step of the way, for every

friendship, every job, every single break in life. By having to work to earn each and every smile you'll ever see.

After all, growth comes from adversity, from frustration. Children don't learn to walk and talk because everything is simply handed to them. They learn to walk because that pretty red thing they want to chew on is too far away. They learn to talk because the big shape that gives them the food isn't giving the food fast enough.
Every single invention ever made was preceded by a problem because, as a race, we're problem solvers. We actually *need* things that we can fix. If life is too easy on us we don't develop the tools to cope.

And why would you develop a personality if things seem to come along just fine without one? Why become interesting and funny and intelligent when people simply flock to you to admire your pretty face? Why change when you're told from birth that you're already perfect?

Sadly, the Beautibubble *will* bursts. It cannot sustain itself. And when it does, even the so-called beautiful people get flung out into the real world, wholly unprepared for existence. ~~Unable to even come up with their own Powerpoint Wake Up lines.~~

So be happy if you actually get the chance to work at this life thing a little.

[sign off]

17

When you're not in love, this entire world doesn't make sense.

I get out of bed feeling slow and lethargic. This could well turn out to be one of my slug-like days.

I did get some sleep but whatever the night is supposed to do to recharge me, it decided not to. Like when a phone-charger cord isn't properly plugged in. I get dressed, already dreading having to interact with other humans in this low energy state, and enter the kitchen. Mom's immediately in my ear about something wildly unimportant.

I try to distract myself with my cell. I check some of apps but there's nothing much to do. Nothing I have the energy for, anyway. But then I notice a little symbol at the top of the screen, something that's not usually there. I click it and my cell tells me I received a message during the night.

bailey: hey you!

My heart stops.

A message from Bailey? Did he really send me something in the middle of the dreaded forty-eight-hour window?

How utterly cool and amazing can one guy be?

I check the timestamp with trembling fingers. The message was sent at 1:54 a.m., which raises all sorts of questions. For instance; did he stay up late and send me this carelessly, or did he wake in the deep, dark night longing to talk to me?

And what does 'hey you!' mean, anyway? Is it one of those '*Hey, you're the one for me!*'s Or is it more of a, '*Hey you, I'm bored, are you there?*'

Mom stares at me.

It seems she's asked a question. I have no hope of answering appropriately so I shrug and start typing.

me: hi, what's up?

Mom rattles some plates to get my attention. "Do you want the last piece of toast or not?"

I almost say yes (in that Pavlovian way I've apparently developed), but then shake my head. I'm surprisingly un-hungry.

My cell buzzes and I almost drop it.

SSJ is online! And he's messaging me back!

77

bailey: what ru up to?

My excitement turns to dread as I realize I'll have to respond in real time. So many possible social pitfalls and so little time to dodge them in.

My thumbs hover over the virtual keyboard, then I remember how effortlessly we talked the other day. How much fun we had. I try to get that feeling back by imagining SSJ sitting across from me right now, smiling and laughing and not at all thinking what a loser I am.

My brain comes unstuck.

me: Oh, I was just teaching some underprivileged capuchin monkeys sign language, how bout u?

bailey: LOL! ;) Taught all my monkeys yesterday, now moving on to armadillos, infinitely more challenging!! ;p

In a perfect world I would've started our messaging relationship on a much funnier note. But it looks like Bailey didn't mind the lame joke. In fact, he replied almost immediately, and that has to be a good sign. Maybe I'm not so bad at this real-time thing after all.

"What's wrong, Willow?"

Mom's staring at me.

I turn over my cell. "Nothing," I say. "Why do you think anything's wrong?"

"You look ill." She touches my forehead. "You're all red and sweaty."

"*You're* all red and sweaty!" I retort, realizing too late how juvenile that sounds.

My cell buzzes in my hand and I quickly get my coat and head out the door. "Sorry! Have to go. See you tonight."

As I unlock my car I notice Mom's following me out. She probably wants to grill me some more. Maybe even stick a thermometer in me or something.

I should've realized sooner that by not moving out I didn't really allow her to start thinking of me as an adult. I should find a way to fix that.

Right now, though, I have to go.

I jump in my car and drive off, quick as I can. When I reach the end of our street, I stop on the side and take out my cell.

bailey: bored out of my skull!!!!
bailey: where are the time lords when you need em?

I check my rear view mirror to make sure no one is about to bumper-kiss me, then type my reply.

me: I heard they're on strike. Something about needing more time off. Ironic, when you think about it..

Yup, I'm on fire. Sure, it's one of those slow-burning, less-than-completely-witty fires, but it's a fire nonetheless.

bailey: true, but sucks 4 me
me: yup. just close up the store and head home, no one will notice :)

After that, Bailey stops messaging. Probably busy with customers. I wait a full seven minutes, signaling what little traffic there is to go around me, then sigh and turn onto the main road.

Almost immediately some idiot cuts me off. Instead of getting upset and placing a curse on him and his offspring, five generations down, I simply smile and wave at him.

I don't think anything can faze me today. After all, I have an SSJ Bailey in my life who could send me a cool message at any moment. It's hard to fault the world right now. On top of that, something strange is happening. For no reason, and completely without my consent, it seems my brain has started a mental conversation with Bailey.

I try to tune it out by turning up the radio.

'*Oh, I love this song!*' the Bailey in my head says.

'*It's* Boys of Summer *by* Don Henley,' I tell him. '*The title came from a book about baseball players having summer flings, although the story in Don's song is much more sad.*'

'*You're so smart,*' SSJ says. '*I never knew that.*'

'*Well, not many people do.*'

I quickly change the channel.

Yes, some part of me (a very large part, in fact) does feel this new development is worrying. This can't be healthy, talking to people in my head. But, well, I kind of like it. So I think I'll allow it for now.

I'll put a time limit on it, though. I'll only talk to the Bailey in my head for five minutes a day.

Six tops.

Promise.

As I expected, I have absolutely no hope of concentrating at work. How can I with all these monumental shifts in my life? Luckily, it doesn't bother me. I'm just biding my time anyway. As soon as lunch rolls around I'll be out of here and back to my *real* life.

I take out my cell and read my messages for the umpteenth time.

"Hey!"

A head pops up over my cubicle wall. It has long dark hair and the exact amount of freckles that men still find attractive.

"Didn't I see you playing with your cell twenty minutes ago?"

It's this account manager called Dorothy-Jane. She's from another department so I don't actually have to listen to a thing she has to says, and she knows it. Nevertheless, she's got this smile on her face as if she's caught me at something. Which she has, I suppose.

"Is that thing glued to your hand or what?"

I shrug and smile. Even though I can feel my face start to burn, her remarks don't bother me as much as they normally would. I'm way too happy right now.

I heard Dorothy-Jane was passed over for promotion twice, and each time happened to coincide with me finding a glaring problem in one of her reports. Instead of thanking me for preventing her ineptitude to be broadcast company-wide, though, she seemed to take it personally. In fact, I may to consider the fact that she might have made it her personal mission to get back at me for helping her.

"Are you planning to do *any* work today?"

I keep my smile in place. "I'm planning to, yes, but we all know how fast plans can change."

We both gape at my bold response.

"Was there anything else?" I ask pleasantly.

Dorothy-Jane frowns, then walks away.

I congratulate myself on staying so polite. I guess I feel for her. After all, she's unlikely to have an SSJ in her life. If she did, she wouldn't be so stressed. If she was getting cool, fun messages at all times of the day, she'd be a different person.

In fact, everybody should always be at most ten minutes away from receiving a cool, fun message. You're only pretending to be alive without that.

I re-read SSJ's messages five more times.

Then another twenty.

Then I finally put my cell away, deep in thought. Could he actually be gunning for the position of being my boyfriend?

18

bailey: so, when r u coming to the store again?
me: why? I'm not sure you deserve to see me
bailey: I do! I'm, like, totally cool, remember? :P
me: not when you talk like that ;)
bailey: hey, i was doing a hipster voice in my head, you should've heard it
me: but I didn't.

Truth is, I'm on my way right now.

I'll be at the nut store in minutes, if this idiot in front of me will just disengage his parking brake and step on the accelerator. I mean, what kinds of speeds are these supposed to be? Old ladies are going to jog past any minute.

I stop at a light and actually feel time wasting away.

My cell buzzes again and I fish it out.

bailey: why do so many of my customers look like Patty and Selma from the Simpsons?
me: them's the breaks, my dear
bailey: seriously, every one of them is short and round!
me: well, it's a popular model and easy to maintain
bailey: sure, but just once I'd like to serve a supermodel or something. I mean, that _could_ happen, right?
me: sure, but the supermodels are probably only half as interesting as the Selmas. Who needs to develop an interesting inner life if they look as if Da Vinci carved them out of marble on one of his extra good days?
bailey: that's a long sentence ~~
me: yup, but probably true

Traffic starts moving again and I put my cell away. I manage to overtake the parking-break-idiot and actually end up making it to the mall in record time. In the parking garage I do another quick check of my cell before getting out.

bailey: aren't u supposed to be working?
me: u should talk!
bailey: hey, I don't have customers, but u get paid by the hour, right?
me: tru, u don't want to know how much your messges have cost so far
bailey: damn.. should I feel guilty?
me: just enough to agree to another lunch with me :P
bailey: I believe I owe that debt to your clients, Madam, not to u
me: ah, so true

bailey: but seriously, I think without u I would've gone mad already
me: what makes you think you haven't?
bailey: 'kay… so is that supposed to be a compliment or an insult?
me: could be a compliment, but don't let it go to ur head
bailey: either way, ur a bad influence on me!
me: of course I am (but why do U think so?)
bailey: I don't think i've ever written this much in one day :) :)
me: c, u cannot live without me ;)
bailey: sure – I'm rolling my eyes at you right now, can u tell?

I have to get a move on or my lunch break will be over before I even get to the store. I stash my cell and get out, hurry towards the escalators. I get off at the top and I spot someone vaguely familiar coming my way. She's tall and blond and, even though I can't quite place her, I instinctively know I don't want to talk to her. I rack my brain trying to recall who she is while simultaneously keeping my head down to make sure we don't accidentally make eye contact.

'Who is this woman?' I ask the Bailey in my head.

'Maybe a friend or a colleague?'

'No, I'm pretty sure I don't know her from work.'

'One of your mom's friends?'

'Nope, way too young.'

I move to the left of the walkway, pretending to browse shop windows. I'm only a few doors from the nut store so maybe I can make it inside unseen. From the corner of my eye, though, I spot the woman doing the exact same thing. She's moved to her right and now we're back on a collision course.

'What a weirdo!' SSJ blurts out.

'Yeah, what's wrong with her?'

I pick up my pace. For some reason I feel it's vitally important that I reach the store before the collision point. Then, as the woman comes closer, I finally recognize her.

It's that weird green eye that gives her away.

And that grey one.

This is my fan, Chloe.

I try to slip into the store unseen but Chloe cuts me off, stepping into the store herself. I have this horrible *a-ha!* moment where I realize it must've been Chloe who was feeding my wake-up lines to Bailey.

I can't believe she's been so bold: using *my* lines in *my* mall on *my* guy!

I take a deep breath and remind myself that it probably doesn't matter. She's going head to head with her master here. Her creator. That green-eyed freak of misconstrued advice is doomed to fail.

Chloe spots me too and a look crosses her face. She knows what's happening here. She picks up her pace and we end up charging the nut store counter full speed. A measure of not-so-accidental shoving follows. But, even though we arrive at the counter more or less simultaneously, I still feel victory is mine. SSJ makes eye contact with me first.

"There you are!" he says. "Guess I deserve to see you after all?"

A surge of pride goes through me. It electrifies my body and I take a moment to smirk at Chloe. She has no idea how deeply Bailey and I are connected already. We're over a hundred quirky messages into… well… into some kind of relationship.

And that's a big deal. That's a real thing.

"I guess you do," I say. "Or maybe I just miss my peppered Brazils."

SSJ Bailey doesn't get a chance to react, Chloe cuts in rudely. "Hey Bailey," she says, "that's a great shirt."

Bailey looks at her. "Thanks, Chlo."

Chlo?

He calls her Chlo?

Wasn't Chloe short enough? And why does he know her name anyway?

"Yeah, that pattern is so safe and generic," she continues, "it'd make a really great tablecloth."

I cringe. That's another one of my wake-up lines. She didn't even bother to change it to fit it to the situation!

Bailey is dumbstruck, insulted. I grin. Taken down by her own treachery, what an amateur. Clearly Chloe didn't gauge the mood correctly and now my victory is cemented in stone. Serves her right for stealing yet another one of my lines.

But then SSJ smiles. "Hey!" he says. "My grandmother designed this shirt especially for me. Don't be bad."

Damn!

And I really don't care for the way he said 'bad'. He made it sound way too good. For a second I consider explaining exactly how bad Chloe really is. How she's feeding him scripted lines that she didn't even script herself. How she doesn't deserve his attention, doesn't deserve his smile, doesn't even deserve to have her name start with a capital letter!

But I can't tell SSJ. Not without revealing some pretty bad things about myself. (Like how I'm giving away perfectly good wake-up lines on YouTube before ever using them on him – and he deserves original lines.)

So, instead, I just say, "Don't mind him, Bai. She was actually born without a working sense of style. It's a terrible affliction. Apparently it affects one in seven point two women. I'm actually thinking of starting a charity. We can beat this thing if we all work together."

But Bailey doesn't hear. He's showing chloe his ring. She's asked him something about it and now she's touching his hand.

She's Touching His Hand!

I don't feel well.

"Oh, I almost forgot," Bailey says. "I was going to get you those Brazils." He finally reclaims his hand and disappears to the back.

chloe grins at me. At least I think she does. I can't be sure because I'm studying the lettering on the store window. It's really intricate work. Very delicate. I wonder if it was a manual job or some kind of sticker affair.

Less than a minute later Bailey returns with my nuts.

"Thanks, Bai," I say. "Perfectly done, as always."

"No problem," he says. "By the way, it looks like clear skies for the rest of the week."

"Great."

Thanks for that really, really short weather report.

I try to think of something else to say, something to remind him that I'm the one he's been messaging – but am I the *only* one? – but nothing comes to mind. This whole messy situation has rattled my brain out of alignment.

Meanwhile, chloe-with-no-capital-letter cuts back in, asking Bailey about his ring again, and flipping her hair in that way I've told all my viewers to never, ever do.

She's really taking all of my advice the exact wrong way.

"You're so weird," I hear Bailey tell her.

"And proud of it," she says, smiling moronically. "My brain simply doesn't operate according to expected parameters."

Which is a mangled version of something I've said in another video.

I look impatiently at Bailey. As he chats away with chloe, I suddenly feel invisible again. All the work I've done these last months to drop my cloak of invisibility seems to have been negated.

I guess I'm supposed to leave but I don't want to. I want to stay and talk to Bailey, get him back into that messaging-mode where he and I talk effortlessly and no one else in the world seems to matter. I want to be the last to leave the store – way, way after chloe. Sadly, I have no idea how to make that happen. And I have no obvious reason for still being here, either. On top of that, chloe's sneakily stepped in front of me and now I look really out of place. I find myself standing to the side as if I'm listening in on their private conversation.

I'm out of options. It appears chloe has won this round.

I turn and leave the store. I'm not even fully aware of walking back to my car. The Bailey in my head does his best to console me.

'Don't worry about all that,' he says. *'You're not going to sulk now, are you?'*

'Of course not,' I tell him. *'But I was really looking forward to talking to you and you made me feel completely invisible.'*

'I was only being professional. I didn't actually want *to talk to that weird woman, I just* had *to because she's a customer.'*

'Meanwhile, you're calling her Chlo for some reason…'
SSJ Bailey sighs. *'Well, you know, I probably couldn't remember her full name.'*
That's a possibility. A definite possibility.
I head back to work and start on a new script.

YouTube script:

I've been thinking about instinct lately. That thing where birds somehow know to fly south for winter, and mother bears know to protect their cubs while father bears go hunting. I'm beginning to wonder whether humans have overlooked something. With all the advanced thinking we do, all the planning and strategizing, aren't we missing the point completely?

Lions hunt deer, beavers build dams, but neither sit around to discuss strategies with their friends beforehand, and they certainly don't look for HowTos on YouTube. All of it is instinct. They're born with everything they need to survive in their environment already built in.

But what do we do? What do we use our larger, more sophisticated human brains for? We use them to come up with complex concepts to precede all of our actions. Concepts like mistrust and worry and fear. And not just the kind of fear that is helpful, like the fear of poisonous spiders and long winters, no, we keep ourselves busy with made-up fears that need yet more concepts to curb them. Concepts like insurances, pensions, and aggressive bumper stickers.

We have definitely developed an acute fear of having less than others, of people taking all the stuff we don't actually need but feel entitled to. And we've even developed a fear for things that may or may not happen in some distant, extrapolated future. This fear, in turn, creates social diseases like hatred, inequality, crime. It fosters the further need for artificial protection structures such as police, government, a penal system.

Yay for the human brain.

But what if we stopped overthinking things for just a moment? What if we listened to what instinct tells us to do? After all, our instinct evolved over generations, changing only when needed. And instinct doesn't try to solve problems that don't exist yet.

For instance, how do boys and girls interact before their giant brains kick in?

If they liked us, boys pull our hair. They hide our lunchboxes.
And if we like them back, we gossip about them and pass notes in class.

That was always our first instinct. So maybe that kind of behavior is actually part of our genetic code. Hardwired into our survival instinct. It could very well be in our species' best interest to do these things, activating something that's buried deep within our primal brainstems.

So, instead of overthinking things, maybe we should just observe little tikes in the playground.

~~Actually, I'm not really sure about this.~~

[sign off]

19

I'm not sure I'll be recording my instinct script after all. It needs more investigation and I have to be way more careful with what I post from now on. Not only is chloe-with-no-capital-letter likely to use whatever I say to dig her claws deeper into my SSJ Bailey, but I've also noticed some pretty weird comments under my videos (turns out, you get idiots everywhere, even on the internet).

One of the really baffling comments is from a follower who calls himself OldMan1963. I check back to see if he's commented before and discover he's a fairly regular contributor. And all of his comments so far have been, well, a little off.

I probably wouldn't even have noticed him if he hadn't sent me a private message. I've been debating heavily whether or I should open it or not.

Sometimes people write weird stuff that can really mess you up, so you have to be careful. Then again, I'm reasonably safe at this end of what is more or less an anonymous connection. And I can always stop reading if it starts to creep me out.

I stare at my inbox a moment longer, still debating the issue, then realize I'm going to let my curiosity win out eventually. The only real question is how much time I'm going to waste convincing myself that it's not such a bad idea after all.

A deep breath, just for good measure, just to show my subconscious that I know I'm getting into *something* right now, and then I click on the message.

Hey Willow, how's life?
I've been trying hard to get in touch with you. I found your TV channel on the world wide web and it looks great. I always knew you'd land on your feet. I'd like to meet with you if you feel up to it.

Dad

I glare at the message in utter disbelief.

At first glance it almost looks as if the entire time I thought Dad was dead but secretly hoped he was alive and checking up on me, he was actually alive and secretly checking up on me.

But looks can be deceiving. This could just as easily be someone pretending to be my dad.

Then again, who even knows he's missing? I don't share any personal details on my channel. And what would be the point of impersonating him anyway?

The sad thing is, I have no idea if this even sounds like him. I have nothing to compare his message to. Not so much as a Christmas card or a farewell note. I don't even know if it's physically possible for him to write me.

Mom isn't much help, either.

"It's probably just one of those dangerous computer errors," she warns me after I bound down the stairs to show her my tablet.

"What dangerous computer errors?"

"You know, you're looking for pictures of cats sitting on pandas and suddenly the screen goes black and there's a message saying you have to pay to unlock your computer."

"A virus?" I glare at her. "You really think a virus wrote me a message saying it's my dad?"

"Could be."

"A virus can't follow your channel, leave you comments, and then tell you that it wants to meet up..."

"I think it can." Mom hands me back my tablet, she's hardly looked at the message. "You should install one of those virus-murderers," she says. "They have them now. Maybe even for your weird flat-computer."

"And what would be the point? What would this semi-sentient virus of yours stand to gain? It's not asking me for my credit card or anything."

"Not *yet*," Mom says.

"Right. So it wants to meet me in person to hit me up for money."

"They're smart little programs," Mom says. "Maureen had a virus that knew her email *and* her number. It stalked her for months!"

I sigh and shut down my tablet. "Look, I only have one simple question, alright? Is Dad dead or not?"

Mom shrugs.

"Come on, did he die or didn't he?"

"It's hard to say," she mumbles. "Whatever happened, I'm sure he's dead by now. I have to start on dinner."

She walks away.

"Mom!"

"What?" Mom whirls round. "What do you want me to say, Willow? He vanished, okay? He just walked out. He never called, he never wrote, he never visited. Not once. You are not going to contact him!"

I'm momentarily stunned by her fierceness, but I recover. "That's not up to you!" I tell her. "You can't tell me what to do!"

"Maybe not," she says, her voice small again, shaky even. "Maybe you're too old for that, but I'm still your mother, and I won't let him hurt you any more than he already has."

She turns, but not before I spot a glint of moisture in the corners of her eyes.

This time I let her go. I don't know what else to do.

Or even think.

I head up to my studio where time passes in a blur. At some point I look out the window and notice it's dark out. I've lost another chunk of time. My tablet lies on my desk and its battery indicator blinks near-empty. There are remnants of thoughts in my head hinting at where the time might have gone. Some of them are of Dad, of him maybe being in prison. Not for a crime, but for doing something good and upsetting the wrong people. Maybe he had to break contact with us for our own protection. Everything he's done since was to keep us safe.

That's so like me. I'm way too positive. I'm always seeing the good in people. I have to stop doing that.

I check my tablet. It's open on my YouTube inbox so I guess I've also spent some time re-reading Dad's message.

Was he really following me online?

Even if he was, though, he can't have been doing it long. Not as long as I've been wanting him to. I've been vlogging for less than a year so it's not like he's been tracking me since he left. It's not like he's been doing whatever he could to find me, working with detectives and the FBI for years and years.

Sure, Mom and I moved a few times, there was so little money, but we were never hard to find. We stayed in the city. In the same area. So what kept him from sending me a birthday card?

I look down at the message and I'm tempted to reply. Not because I want to re-initiate contact, but because I have so much to get off my chest.

Do you know I think about you every single day?

Do you know I look for you in the crowd, examining every face to see if you're checking up on me?

How could you do this to us?

How could you forget about me?

I switch off my tablet and connect it to the charger. There is no way this man could give me a satisfying answer. Besides, I had to wait decades for my first message from him, it'd be insane to send him a reply on the very same day.

Why couldn't you just love me?

It doesn't matter. None of it matters. I have my mom, my fans, and, most importantly, I have my SSJ Bailey. I don't need anyone else. In fact, it's about time I sent Bailey a message. I've punished him long enough for being so callously friendly to chloe.

me: Hi! There r some important weather changes we should discuss

It doesn't take long for a reply to arrive and I immediately feel that curious little tingle shoot through my body.

bailey: Really? Let's hear it!
me: not safe to discuss over an open channel. let's meet in person!
bailey: K. when?

So far so good. I take a deep breath and compose my killer reply. I have to back-track a few times because I keep fudging it up.

me: tell you hwat, since I'm such a cool customer I'm going to clear my schedule for Saturday nite. ur one lucky, lucky dude!
bailey: who r u calling dude? how about we discuss during lunch monday?
me: it can't wait till monday. show of hands for sat nite
bailey: but lunch is the traditional time for weather reports, no?
me: doesn't matter, we're starting a new tradition
bailey: why tho? I can't make it sat nite
me: ah… sure?
bailey: pretty sure :) bsy with friends

Busy with friends? Seriously? We haven't been on an almost-certainly-a-date in ages and he'd still rather hang out with his lame friends? Who cancels the date of a lifetime for their boring old friends? You hang out with friends on weekdays, if you really have to, you don't waste a perfectly good Saturday night on them!

>   **me:** they'll understand, don't worry
>   **bailey:** understand what?
>   **me:** that ur canceling for something more important
>   **bailey:** fnny grl! no thanks, looking forward to seeing my friends

I realize I'm shaking. My heart pounds in my ears. His messages almost make it sound like I mean nothing to him, like I'm just a fun little distraction during work hours.

I quickly move over to my bed because I think I'm having some kind of attack. I'm heavy and lightheaded at the same time. The room is spinning. I can hardly type out my reply.

>   **me:** fine, good luck with ur friends. gotto go. I'm ill

This might be it. The big one. There's something seriously wrong with me and I may not last till morning.

As I lay down I notice I can hardly hold my tablet long enough to check for a reply, which is just as well, because SSJ doesn't send me any more messages.

20

There's definitely something about shoe-shaped objects that activates the pleasure centers of the female brain.

I'm still alive the next morning, sadly enough, and without Bailey to message me (he still hasn't replied to my last, snarky, message) the week creeps by very slowly. Once again time itself seems broken, or at least suffering from a generous amount of sand stuck in its wheels.

When Saturday rolls around I'm starting to go crazy so I take Mom up on her offer to take me shopping. My shoes are scuffed and have to be replaced before I show my face (feet) at work again.

As fragile morning light filters in through the glass ceiling, our footsteps echo around the deserted mall. Mom's up ahead, walking way too fast for someone her age, and I'm trundling after, my feet already killing me. We've covered over ten stores and the day hasn't even seen its first nine o'clock. I never noticed that half the mall is actually shoe-stores.

"Willow," Mom calls over her shoulder. "Stop dragging your feet."

"I'm not dragging my feet, I'm observing generally accepted pedestrian speeds."

"I'm observing generally unacceptable nonsense," Mom retorts. She hikes up her pace.

"Where's the fire?" I call after her. "That's all I want to know."

We pass the food court and I suddenly feel like sitting down and munching on something terribly bad for my body and terribly good for my mood and taste buds. I don't even slow down, though, because I know my powers of persuasion are no match for Mom's current level of enthusiasm. She's treating this like some kind of Shoe Emergency.

A Shoetastrophy.

"These stores will still be here in an hour," I tell her. "They'll still be here in a thousand years, long after our society has collapsed and the second wave of cavemen takes over."

"Always complaining," Mom says. "Let's check in here."

She disappears into a store I've never seen before. In fact, I could swear it appeared only a second ago.

I follow her inside.

Of course I know that, as a woman, shopping should be my first love. Shoe shopping especially. I was at the meeting, the one where all women got together and unanimously decided to dedicate their lives to the pursuit of cute footwear. I'm aware of being the odd one out, yet again. But, well, I never got that thing, that feeling that other women seem to get when they find one pair of shoes – or jeans, or a top – that looks slightly better than another.

That part of me is broken.

Or it was never really there in the first place.

So it's good that Mom wants to help, I just wish she wasn't so fanatical about it. I worry she's been waiting for an opportunity to go shopping with her daughter for so long that she won't allow it to end. Ever.

Mom finds a pair of reasonably looking walking shoes, but their soles are thick with nonsense that has air and foam passing for *technology*.

"It's really modern," she says, waving them in my face. "What do you think?"

"I think you're mistaking ugly for modern."

"Just try them on," she says. "You might like them. They have Superior Airflow (tm) technology."

Exactly.

I ask her to go find something else. Which she does, practically skipping along the aisle as she returns the airflow monstrosities to where she found them and checks out their direct neighbors.

"You might as well skip this whole rack," I call after her. "All these shoes are entirely too, as you put it, modern."

Mom shakes her head at me and moves out of sight.

I take out my cell and check for messages from SSJ.

Nothing.

I really hope he didn't take my last message the wrong way. I didn't mean to sound bitchy, I just wanted to point out how weird it was that he'd prefer to spend all his time with people who are, very fundamentally, not me. And besides, Saturdays are looong. If he really wanted to see me he could easily have re-allocated one or two of its many hours.

"What about these?"

Mom waves another pair of shoes in my face.

"They're very boring and black," I say. "So that's good."

"Try them on."

"I would, but the heels are too high."

"All shoes have heels."

"Not like this they don't. I won't be able to walk on them comfortably."

Mom sighs. "They're not supposed to be *comfortable*, Willow," she says. "They're supposed to *look good*."

Yet another one of those things the women decided at the meeting.

I really should've spoken up.

"I'll have to walk on them all day at a job I already hate," I tell her. "I'm not adding this discomfort to my torture list."

Mom shrugs and disappears.

I check my cell again.

No messages.

I wonder if maybe I should break the radio silence, but I wonder it only briefly. It would undermine everything I've said and done so far.

I hear Mom ask a sales clerk about Superior Airflow(tm) technology and share a bored eye roll with a chubby guy down the aisle. He's wearing a Star Trek t-shirt with a suspicious stain on the shoulder and I quickly decide to assume it's just coffee.

Chubby is around my age and is also shoe shopping with his mom. I know this because, 1) I spot an older lady just ahead of him checking out a pair of purple sneakers, and 2) there's a significant deal of resignation about his body language.

I feel bad for him. Like me, he should have a cell filled with messages sent by an admirer. Everybody should. We deserve it.

He'll be okay, though. Sooner or later he'll go to a comic book convention, meet a girl with a stained Dr. Who backpack, and they'll get married and have a bunch of kids with stained Sponge Bob socks. And, who knows, eventually they may even learn to wash at higher temperatures.

I look around. Maybe I can find some shoes myself. It'd really help speed things up. I browse the racks but quickly realize it's hopeless, I don't have any idea where to start. Grouped together all these shoes look weird to me. It's a massive informational overload of rubber, leather, and foam. They'd have to make an app before I could even consider tackling this myself.

Perhaps moms are better equipped to work with this kind of unsorted data.

"What about this one?"

A familiar voice comes from the rack behind me.

"It's got a weird nose. You like weird noses, right? I mean, why else would you have one in the middle of your face?"

I peek between the shelves and spot the owner of the voice. It's *chloe*, my arch nemesis. My sworn rival. And she's holding up a weird looking pair of shoes.

"Come on," she says. "Try these on. For me."

I move some shoes so I can see who she's talking to, then my heart almost stops.

SSJ Bailey isn't out with friends, he's out with *chloe!*

And he's smiling at her!

Looking all goofy and happy.

I feel queasy and look for a place to sit. Luckily there's a shoe-try-on stool beside me. I drop down on it unceremoniously.

"Fine, hand them over," Bailey says.

"Don't be silly. They're horrible. I was only joking. But I'd love to see you in a pair of these. Try them on?"

There's a sigh from chloe when Bailey rejects her new choice. As if she's exasperated. As if being out shoe shopping with Bailey isn't quite special enough for her.

The Bailey in my head tries to calm me down.

'It's nothing,' he tells me. *'I probably ran into her on my way to my friends.'*

I ignore him and concentrate on my breathing.

'Don't be so dramatic. I'm just letting Chlo help me because I feel sorry for her.'

'You're not,' I mumble. *'I can hear the way you're talking to her.'*

'That's just...' He thinks it over. *'That's just because I'm thinking of you. I probably just miss you. As much as you miss me. If not more.'*

But I no longer trust the Bailey in my head. Especially when he tells me to go over there and say hello.

'Don't worry,' he says. *'It'll be fine. Just say Hi! and I will take it from there. We'll get rid of chloe together.'*

Mom suddenly manifests at my feet, her arms full of shoes.

"You're trying all of these on," she announces breathlessly.

She's gone insane. She's turned into a shoe-monster. And, as I'm clearly not feeling well, she might also be a hallucination. But I can't risk her being real and having chloe and Bailey hear us, so I have to get rid of her. Luckily I know exactly what to say to make any version of Mom, real or imagined, disappear.

"I think I just saw a pair of air-Clarks a few racks over," I whisper. "They might be on sale."

Mom disappears like a puff of smoke. Perhaps she wasn't real after all. I shouldn't have worried, though, because, as I lift myself back up, I see that SSJ is way too busy with chloe to notice anyone else.

'Of course I'm not! I'm just too bored to notice anyone, that's all!'

I sneak away.

I have to get out of the store. Or better yet, out of the mall. Or better yet, out of the country.

Mom's standing near the register, checking out a pair of air-Clarks with a half-off sticker on them.

How on earth did she manage to find those?

"Mom," I call out to her, "we're buying whatever you have in your hands right now because we have to get out of here."

Comments:

OldMan1963: (7:42 pm) Kayleigh, I know it's been a long time and how can you be sure this is me, right? But I'm really trying here. Look, I'm even using your world wide web name, see?

Squincyforu: (8:14 am) This channel sucks on so manuy levels. I nevr knew someone could suck so much!!! Well done.. now stop sucking somuch

OldMan1963: (1:42 pm) Are you there?

LoveIsLost: (1:54 pm) K. I've been taking your advice but I'm not having much of luck. Here in my country maybe guys is different. Please help out. Can I tell you about my date and you can overanalyze for hidden flaws?

Kayleigh256: (6:27 pm) Sure, LoveIsLost, go ahead.

Loveislost: (6:29 pm) Ok, so I see guy in club and he very pretty. I know lot of girls will want to have this pretty guy, so I do different from other girls. But he don't react as I expect.

Kayleigh256: (6:31 pm) Can you tell me exactly what you did?

Loveislost: (6:35 pm) Okay so I go up to guy with my hands behind back.
Me: Hello there.
He: Hello woman.
Me: I have something for you.
He: Let me guess, you bought me drink.
Me: No, I bought you puppy.
(I give him puppy)
He: ….
Me: I was thinking, you have lots of drinks, but you do not have puppy.
He: ...
Me: What is wrong, you don't like puppy? Is wrong color?
He: You are giving me dog?
Me: Yes, most puppies is dogs. In fact, all puppies is dogs I think.

Loveislost: (6:39 pm) Then guy goes to talk to other girl. Which is not unusual, I know what that means. But last night I was confused because guy took my puppy. So I guess my question is, K, what it means when guy doesn't want relationship with you but he does want your puppy?

Kayleigh256: (6:40 pm) What country are you from? When you say puppy, you do mean a soft, small animal, right?

Loveislost: (6:42 pm) Yes, puppy is very small and soft.

Kayleigh256: (6:42 pm) So, just to be clear, you brought a small dog to a bar?

Loveislost: (6:43 pm) Of course. Is bad idea to bring big dog to bar. Everyone knows this.

Loveislost: (6:46 pm) K? You still there?

Loveislost: (7:10 pm) K?

WhatsCrck: (9:06 pm) You see the kind of inbred idiots your breading, K!

DissonantMelody: (9:27 pm) You mean "you're breeding" right? I don't think Kayleigh is going around stuffing her followers between slices of bread!

TimyLiz: (9:43 pm) Hehe :) Nice one, Melody!

Loveislost: (10:43 pm) Should I try other animal? Maybe rabbit or hamster? I have magician friend, he can teach me to hide in top hat.

Loveislost: (11:28 pm) Should I wear top hat, K?

OldMan1963: (11:58 pm) Okay, so ask me any question. I'll prove it's me.

21

bailey: hey, sorry I didn't write
bailey: I was craxy busy :p
bailey: r u there?

bailey: have time for a chat?
bailey: hello?
bailey: guess ur busy too :(

bailey: hey, just thought I'd try one more time…
bailey: miss u…

me: hey…
bailey: ah, she's alive, alive I tell you!!
me: so what were you so busy with?
bailey: u know, friends and stuff. u?
me: me? I've been buying shoes…
bailey: ok. good ones?
me: good enough. so how are your friends?
bailey: they're fine
me: have *you* bought any shoes lately?
bailey: actually have. and I have great news too!!
me: I doubt it..
bailey: waht?
me: never mind. what's ur great news?

me: still there?
bailey: sorry, customer, had to get back to real life :(so, what were
we talking about?
me: u had some news
bailey: Oh, yeah! get this: I have a girlfriend! can you believe
that? nerdyoldme with an actual girlfriend? how crazy is that?

bailey: hello?
bailey: u still there?
me: yeah, just had to do something
bailey: u know what would be cool?
me: not really, no
bailey: do you have a boyfriend (you proably do) we shouldgo
on a double date!
me: no thanks
bailey: :p haha. but seriously, it would be crzay fun!

> **bailey:** r u there?

> **bailey:** Hello?

After feeling pretty lethargic for a couple of days I suddenly find the inspiration to write scripts again. A whole series of them, in fact. I write eight scripts in two days, which is definitely a new personal record. But these aren't my usual, insightful, helpful scripts. These scripts are pure evil. They're laced with bad advice and aimed directly at chloe. They're designed specifically to help her destroy her new relationship.

Yup, I'm Evil Cyrano-ing my channel. My reputation be damned, I'm unleashing the beast! Without Bailey there is no Kayleigh256 and Kayleigh256 has to survive in order to continue to save lives. So this is all still for the greater good. Yes, there may be some collateral damage. A few of my followers might get caught in the crossfire, and that's truly terrible, that keeps me awake at night, but, ultimately, it can't be helped. Not right now. If I have any followers with actual boyfriends then I'll have to help them fix the mess I'm about to make later. After I take out chloe.

> **bailey:** willow, u there?
> **bailey:** ur so busy these days, what's up?
> **bailey:** can u guys make it for a double date this friday?

The first evil video explains that, once a guy is officially your boyfriend, you should step up the attention giving. You should be talking to him nonstop, showering him with gifts, hanging on his lip and his arm, and checking up on what he's doing every second of the day.

Basically there's no such thing as too much attention.

Not only do guys love this, they actually *need* it. It's a crucial step in us showing them that we're serious about the relationship. That we're no longer looking around for someone better.

It's time to stop worrying about the guy thinking that you like him more than he likes you. That rule is out the window.

Making sure he knows you've taken yourself off the market is more important right now.

So blow up his cell with messages, then take it away from him every chance you get to check his pictures and other message threads. This will make him feel really secure.

The second evil video talks about the importance of keeping your guy away from his dumb buddies.

It's a classic. It explains that he shouldn't really need anyone else. You should be enough for him. And he certainly doesn't need his friends reminding him of all the girls he's missing out on now he's in a relationship. He doesn't need them taking him to bars and introducing him to all sorts of potential sleeping partners.

His friends are nothing but trouble. No matter what their intention, their effects on your relationship are neutral at best and negative at worst. So keep those dumb guys away.

As it turns out, it's not that hard to make this kind of advice sound logical to the female mind.

Then I do a video on '*Flirting with other guys in front of him*'.

Obviously this is the next logical step after making sure that He knows you're off the market. Once he's secure in your relationship, he'll start taking you for granted. That's just the way it goes. He'll stop paying attention to you and start noticing other girls. He's a hunter at heart, and once he's tamed you, you're no longer a challenge for him.

So what do you do? You kick out your hooves from time to time, let him know you're still a flight risk. And you do this by flirting very subtly with other guys in front of him. It'll show him that other men are still interested in you, and that they're ready to step up if he doesn't.

Of course, I forget to explain the bit on how to flirt without looking tacky and unhappy with the relationship. And I certainly don't mention how bad it will look if you're shot down by another guy in front of *Him*. How devastating that double whammy of disrespect and undesirability is.

Yes, chloe, this is what happens when you make me use my brain for evil.

> **bailey:** hey! come get a coffee with me and Chlo?
> **bailey:** we're at the mall right now. just know you'll like her
> **bailey:** u have so much in common

Of course I do miss my SSJ. I miss our chats and that intense feeling of being in an almost-relationship. Of being on the cusps of something new and beautiful that'll change my life forever. But I really can't talk to him right now. Not until his thing so-called relationship with chloe starts showing some cracks.

So far, though, for all my brilliantly evil insights, for all my hard work on the dark side, there's been no change in Bailey's demeanor. He still seems more than happy with chloe. Which really makes me wonder whether chloe is giving it her all. I mean, is she even paying attention to my posts? Am I not clear and destructive enough? Or has she stopped watching my channel altogether?

Meanwhile, I have all these weird images popping into my head. Sometimes I see them fighting, throwing stuff at each other and screaming their heads off – chlo can barely hold on to her illegal catch. But other, more frequent, times I think they're way too busy sleeping together for chlo to watch my channel.

> **bailey:** serioulsy, did ur cell break? ;p talk to me!

Strangely, my channel has become much more popular. Not only have my views shot up, I'm getting more followers every day. I haven't seen this much growth on my channel since, well, forever.

Which makes no sense, I've just been spewing garbage.

In any other universe this kind of growth would be good, but in this one, at this moment, it only means that the collateral damage is much higher than I'd anticipated. Women and girls are dropping like flies all over the internet, wounded and unable to fend for themselves. The one nerdy girl who was supposed to be in their corner has betrayed them. Thrown them to the wolves.

I really don't think I can't push this thing any further. Even if it was working (which it isn't), I'd have to pull the plug.

No more Evil Cyrano-ing for me.

This isn't worth it.

I have to try something else.

> **me:** Hey Bai
> **me:** srry I hvn't been in touch. soo bsy with my guy friends
> **bailey:** hey ur back! No prblm. Was pretty bsy myself ;)
> **me:** Yeah, I just got so mch going on right now, it's insnae
> **bailey:** cool :) ok, let's talk tomorrow then, gotto go
> **me:** wait!
> **me:** are u still there?
> **me:** Bai?

So much for making him jealous and having him miss me. Even subconsciously he refuses to realize how boring his life is without me.

I thought I'd shake him awake by showing him that he's been feeling so good, not because of this so-called girlfriend, but because he had me in his life. Everything just seems better against the backdrop of our cool messages. He was just mixing up the pleasure signals in his head, attributing them to chloe and her stolen material instead of to me.

But even that's not working.

He just can't see it.

I decide to take down my last eight posts and move on to plan B.

YouTube Script:

Whatever happens, remember that we're all connected. We're all just expressions of universal energy. At the quantum level, we'll never have to miss anyone. We are together forever.

Video #83 by *Kayleigh256*. **Views: 234**

Comments:

DissonantMelody: (12:27 pm) Where are you, K? We miss you!!

Loveislost: (14:18 pm) What is going on? Why no posts for weeks? You have to tell me what to do next.

OldMan1963: (15:15 pm) Are you getting any of my messages? I don't know if I'm doing this right. Willow, if you want me to leave you alone, if that's what you truly want, just tell me...

GuyFLx: (9:36 pm) About time. Can't tell you how happy \i am that she stopped posting.

Vogon43: (10:28 pm) She finally realized how stupid her channel is!

DissonantMelody: (14:27 pm) Whatever's going on, you take your time, K. We'll be here right here when you return.

So that's how I got into my sort-of, kind-of breakup, Alice.

I hope you'll agree that none of it was really my fault. I was always so careful, so guarded, but I caved when I thought I got the right signals. I let myself be tricked into believing that I could have a nice guy and a normal life.

The little girl you knew before would never have let that happen. But they got into her head, Alice. They made her believe that it was just a little more difficult for her, but not impossible.

It's a mean thing to do to a person.

But that's all water under the bridge now. I think you'll agree that I had no choice but to divert all my mental resources away from designing the perfect seduction strategy and on to something more important. After all, in most cases that kind of thing happens on its own, anyway, without people even trying.

So I left that beaten internet path and focused my efforts on a new goal. I was going to scientifically determine how to get over someone with the highest degree of efficiency.

Yup. I was going to crack the most elusive code ever. Solve the one problem that we'll all suffer from at some point in our lives.

Dear, dear Alice. I'm not kidding myself. I know you'll probably never read this. I know you won't sit down with my letters and think about me, that's just not in the cards. But writing this still helps me. I like to pretend you're here with me and I'm telling you everything that's going on in my life.

So let me tell you what happened next…

22

I'm sitting in this little café on the other side of town, trying my best to put my thoughts in order. My dad sits across from me, smiling amiably, and I can't help but notice how much older he looks than I expected him to. There are so many tiny lines crisscrossing his face and he barely has any hair left. Also, he looks too little like me while at the same time looking too much like me.

It's hard to explain.

"I'm glad you came," he says.

I look out the window. None of this feels real. It feels like Christmas and Armageddon just fell on the same day. Am I supposed to be happy? Sad? Angry? I really have no idea.

And I wish I'd prepared a little better. Sure, I had almost two decades to get ready for this moment, but I honestly didn't think this day would ever come, so I never gave it any serious thought. Not the way I usually give things.

A waitress comes over and places two coffees on our table. This makes me even more uncomfortable. I don't drink coffee so Dad will have to drink both cups, or return one, or try to sell one to another table, which I think is illegal.

I take a breath and remind myself the fate of the coffees isn't important.

"Why did you just walk out on us?" I blurt out.

Because, why not start with the big question?

Dad looks puzzled, as if he hadn't expected that question. "Well," he says after a very long moment, "that's just the thing. I didn't." He searches for words. "In my mind, that's not what happened."

"But somehow Mom and I ended up living alone for almost twenty years."

We sit quietly while Dad pulls one of the coffees towards him, blowing on it before taking a careful sip. "Here's the thing," he says. "I just didn't stop, you know? I was on this ride through my life, having a good old time, and then your mom suddenly decided to pull over and have babies, put up a white picket fence." He gives me a meaningful look. "I wasn't even close to my destination, Willow. I mean, I couldn't just stop in the middle of nowhere, could I?"

He takes another sip of his coffee before putting it down on the table.

"I didn't walk out on you guys," he says. "Your mother just decided, all on her own, that she was going to stop traveling with me."

Anger wells up. He isn't making sense. "What the hell's that supposed to mean?"

Dad shrugs. "On some level I guess I just wasn't ready. I never got the chance to think about it, you know? To make my own decision. It was all just shoved down my throat. We never sat down and discussed getting boring jobs, settling down in a shitty house, and dying slowly in one place."

I stare at him.

"Willow," he says, "you know her. She's always doing stuff like that, not including anyone in her decisions. She changed our whole lives in one day, everything we'd planned, was I just supposed to roll over and play dead? It was my life too."

I look out the window. Life seems much simpler out there. Is it possible that those people passing by all have easier lives than I do? Could The World simply have decided to be nicer to them? Or am I kidding myself here?

I probably am.

"None of what you're saying makes sense," I say. "You were still my dad. You didn't have to leave me. What did I ever do to you?"

He shrugs and nips at his coffee, and I hate how little this seems to affect him. It's as if he hasn't thought about any of this in years. As if my life, my pain, is just a little anecdote for us to pass the time with.

"If you look at it from my perspective," he says, pulling the second coffee towards him, "you weren't really a person."

"Excuse me?"

"You know what I mean. At that time, you really weren't. You were just something that happened. In a way, I didn't leave *you*, I only left the concept of you. The concept of having a baby."

"But I *wasn't* a baby!" I almost yell at him. "I was ten years old! Of course I was a real person!"

He gives me a look as if I'm deliberately not getting it. "You can't take this personal," he says. "I just had this weird feeling that my life would be over. I still had so much to do."

"Oh, really?" I struggle to keep my anger in check. "So please enlighten me, Dad, what are these great things that you did with your life?"

He gives me another puzzled look. It seems this particular question hasn't come up, either.

"Seriously," I say. "What could you possibly have done with your life that was more important than being someone's only biological father? What was so all-consuming that you couldn't even call me on my birthdays?"

Dad frowns. "What difference would that have made? What would a few minutes of conversation here and there have accomplished?"

"Are you seriously asking me this?"

"Yes. Wouldn't it just have made things worse?" He shoots me a patronizing smile. "Look, Willow, there's no reason to get upset. All this happened years ago and you're smart enough to know we can't change the past. We came here to talk about the future. So let's do that."

My head is spinning.

"I did what was best for all of us. I mean, just look at you now, you turned out great. You're not a criminal, you're not an addict, you have a job and you even have your own TV channel. On the World Wide Web no less. That's global!"

I stare at him. I'm completely overwhelmed by the intensity with which he believes his own bullshit.

There's nothing for me to say here. Not a single word. In fact, I don't think the words even exist that could penetrate Dad's armor of kinked logic.

The only thing I can do is get up and leave. That's the only action that makes sense.

"Please don't say I turned out the way I did because of you," I hiss at him, moving my chair back. "I turned out this way *in spite* of you!"

I leave the table without looking back.

I almost don't seek out the waitress to pay for the second coffee.

That's how upset I am.

When I'm back out in the street, something odd happens. At first I expect Dad to come running after me. Stopping me in my tracks to tell me he was joking. Or that he's finally realized how much he loves me and misses me. But that's not what happens.

Of course it's not.

What actually happens is that my feet get stuck. The searing heat has turned a patch of tarmac to a thick, pasty gum that catches my sneakers.

I struggle to get out but with every move my feet sink deeper.

This is too ridiculous for words.

Meanwhile, a group of kids has formed a circle around me. I immediately recognize them from my old high school. They're the ones who tortured me on a regular basis. They laugh now, too. I reach out to Gwen, the short girl with the pigtails who wasn't quite so mean before, and I beg her to help me out, or at least bring me some clothes, because, for some reason, I've forgotten mine.

I'm stuck in the tarmac in my underwear.

But Gwen doesn't help. She just points and laughs and sticks out her tongue.

Which is when I wake up, drenched in sweat.

I stare up at the ceiling for hours, watching shadows turn slowly to daylight, and I wonder what that dream meant. What my subconscious was trying to tell me. Was it warning me? Was it telling me to never, ever get my hopes up?

23

Here's a little test: *Does every song on the radio remind you of him?**

*) If so, snap out of it! Do you really think this is deep and meaningful? Do you really
believe he'll sense it if you wallow *deep* enough?

It's 11 a.m. and my colleagues start to gravitate towards the coffee area.
The resulting noise is similar to the buzzing of a beehive, it's the sound
of people trying to appear much happier than they really are – an over-
compensatory reaction that I'm sure happens in offices all over the
world. Lame jokes and boring anecdotes are suddenly laughed at loudly
due to a malfunction deep within the human brain. It's a defunct
survival mechanism that tells us that if we laugh along and try to fit in,
others won't turn on us and eat us.

At least, that's what I think it is.

I stare at my screen, where I've been trying to make 'work' happen for
a couple of hours now. Somehow, though, it's just not happening. Every
second that passes turns out to be one of those seconds in which I
didn't quite do anything.

While the beehive buzzes away I gently move my arm to make sure
it's still functioning. I wriggle my fingers and shift my shoulders. There
don't seem to be any mechanical problems. I should be able to perform
basic tasks such as typing and mouse clicking – and isn't that the bulk of
my professional existence anyway?

In fact, now I think about it, most of my adult life has been about the
pressing of plastic keys and the moving of a plastic mouse. So does this
mean that my value as a human can be expressed in terms of how well
I've moved and pressed said bits of plastic? And, if so, does this mean
that my headstone should read something like: *Here lies Willow, by Jove this
woman could click! We'll miss her dearly, especially the way she was able to ctrl-s
Save her work without interrupting her typing.*

I push the thought away and realize several more seconds have
passed.

And I've used them to do more nothing.

I've managed to waste even the wasting of time.

I'm slightly amazing that way.

"Hey, you're here!"

Gary peers over my cubicle wall, apparently surprised to see me sitting
where I always sit. "Weren't you going on holiday?"

I'm lost. "On holiday?"

"Yeah, I didn't think you'd be back so soon. Where did you go?"

"Do you mean, where did I go four weeks ago?"

Gary frowns. "No," he says. "Didn't you say you were going to Florence this week?"

I cringe. I function so much better when people leave me to myself. "No, sir, I've been right here, working on the quarterly reports."

"You sure?"

"Pretty sure, yes."

"Didn't you send me an email about going to Florence?" He looks at me as if I might still come to my senses and remember I'm supposed to be out of the country.

I shake my head.

"So why haven't you been to any of the belly-feeling meetings this week?"

"I was at every single one."

"Come on." He shoots me an annoyed look. "You definitely weren't there yesterday."

"I was. I was standing right next to you."

"You were?"

This is a worrying development. I can't have him thinking I've been slacking off, not when my slacking off period is only just about to start.

"I gave you the Krestmont report, remember? You signed off on it, told me it was good work."

Gary sucks some air in between his teeth. "That was you? I thought Dorothy-Jane was on the Krestmont account?"

"Nope, that was me."

"Well, I suppose I should talk to Dorothy-Jane, sort this whole thing out."

"Kay." I return my attention to my screen but realize there's nothing going on there. I was going to type a bit, just to look busy, but there's nothing open to type into. No spreadsheet, no document, no nothing. I'd type away but I have no idea what would happen.

Gary finally turns to go, then turns back again. "Wait," he says. "Then who went to Florence?"

"I wouldn't know." I quickly scribble some random numbers on a pad by my keyboard. I put down a six and cross out a twenty-seven that was already there. Yup, this is pretty professional looking right here. "I've been way too busy working to pay attention to people's holidays."

"Have it your way," he says. "But you'll want to talk to human resources, someone may have told them you were on holiday."

With that he walks away.

I guess I should go after him, just to make sure that Dorothy-Jane, with her perfect-freckle-count-face and her possible personal vendetta against me, doesn't take credit for my report, but I can't move. I can't move because I realize I don't really care. I simply, to put it very crass, don't give a fuck. My fuck-giving level fails to surpass the movement-requirement-threshold and so I'm stuck in my chair.

The sad truth is, nothing that happens in this office ultimately matters. In the history of humanity, it won't make a blip of difference.

In fact, I might as well drop what I'm doing right now and work on a script. I've been thinking about writing a new script for a while now. A script containing information that every person in the world will need at some point in their lives. Not just people like me, and not just women, but everybody. At some point we'll all need to know: '*How to get over The One.*'

It's hard to even imagine the power of such a script. How deeply it'd impact global society, how high it'd raise human productivity. If no one is ever left pining for the One for more than, say, a few hours, then our planet would reach new, unknown heights.

So far, though, I've got nothing.

I don't even know where to start. I'm not even sure there really *is* a cure, other than letting obscene amounts of time pass.

(Time that, of course, will be wasted.)

But I do know one thing: it's our own brains that make us feel miserable. Our own brains that make us sad and lonely, forcing us to wallow away day after day. And that doesn't seem right. We don't just own our brains, we don't just control them, we *are* our brains. We should get a say in how they make us feel. It's our fundamental right to be able to pick and choose our feelings.

We just need to figure out how to do this.

"Did you bring me any cheese?"

Wilson shoots me an innocent smile over my cubicle wall. He's a temp like me, but I've only spoken to him once, I have no idea why he'd think we're on 'bringing each other cheese' terms.

"What cheese?"

"Isn't Florence famous for its cheese?"

That again? Does the whole department think I've been to Florence? "No," I tell him, "I don't think Florence is particularly famous for its cheese, sorry."

Sometimes I think I should start wearing bits of spinach between my teeth, just so people will be even more tempted to leave me to myself.

It'd be like a fashion statement, but in reverse.

"Wooden shoes, then?"

I shake my head. "Wooden shoes don't sound like Florence, either."

Wilson doesn't give up. "How about windmills?"

"If you're asking me if I brought you any windmills, then no, I didn't."

He nods thoughtfully.

"Look, I'm sorry, but I wasn't on holiday."

"Are you sure? Because Gary says you were, so…"

I shake my head. "Nope."

"Ok." He shrugs and saunters off. I take out my cell and check for messages.

Nothing.

There hasn't been anything for days now. It's like I don't even exist.

The coffee area beehive starts to calm down and my colleagues head back to their respective cubicles. I watch them go and wonder how they manage to care so much about their jobs, what they think the point is of all the evaluations and meetings and that slow harrowing climb up the corporate ladder.

It's all so inherently meaningless it's actually scary. It's like everybody else has built up much better defenses against the meaninglessness of life than I have. I know it can't be true, but it really feels like everything on this planet means exactly nothing if you don't have that one special person in your life.

Imagine stocking up on gas, when you don't have a car. Imagine trying to figure out the best brand of tampon, when you're a dude. Imagine buying a nice welcome mat, that's exactly the right material, the right size, the right color, when a tornado has just destroyed your home.

It's totally focusing on the wrong thing, is what I'm saying.

24

Mom wants an update on Bailey when I get home.

"When's your next date?"

I'm not sure how to respond. In fact, I was really looking forward to not ever broaching this subject again. I try to shrug casually as I say, "You know what, we don't have any definite plans as of yet."

Mom's not happy. "Be careful," she says. "You don't want him to cool off. You should always have another date lined up. A man needs to know if he's part of your ongoing plans or he'll start looking around."

I'm not sure how to respond. I'm not sure I want to get into how making a date with my Bailey went from being extremely difficult to completely impossible, and more than a little pointless. And I really don't want to get into how invisible and stupid I feel.

"I think we'll just see each other when we see each other," I tell her. "Anyway, I don't really have time to line up dates and worry about what to wear. I'm a creator. An artist. I have to go with the creative flow, see where it takes me."

Mom shoots me a sad little smile. "So it didn't work out, I'm so sorry Willow. I hope you won't let that get you down. Hey, you know what you should do? You should give Maureen's cousin another call."

That again?

I thought we had a ceasefire?

"I think he just broke up with his new girlfriend," she gives me a nudge. "You won't have to worry about him being too clingy. Just use him for practice."

"Mom!"

"Don't think I don't notice what's been going on," she says. "You've been moping around the house for weeks, locking yourself in your room."

"My Studio," I correct her. "Where I work on my channel."

"But you don't, do you? Not anymore. You haven't put up anything new in a long time."

"What? How do you—"

"It's not healthy, Willow. I know how you get. You over-think things and take everything way too personal. I know you're more fragile than most people, but this isn't healthy. You were doing so well, getting out of the house, finding a job, talking to people, even going on dates. Please don't let this little setback destroy all that. Please don't slip back into—"

"Mom! I'm fine!"

"But you're not." She tries to pinch my cheek, I step out of reach. "I don't want to do this," she says, "but I will if I have to."

"Do what?"

Mom points to the phone. "You're going out on Friday, Willow. Either you make plans or I do."

I try to think of something to say but nothing comes to mind. Or maybe too many things come to mind. I glare at her and head up to my studio.

Mom just doesn't understand. It's as if I was sleeping for years, letting life pass me by, living on autopilot, and then I met Bailey and I suddenly woke up, I suddenly noticed all these emotions and colors and this weird thing people call happiness. But then chloe came along and trampled everything.

So these are my choices: feel intense pain, or put myself back to sleep.

But I don't want to give up on all these wonderful new things I almost had. I don't want to go back to sleep.

I take out my tablet and boot it up. It's time to work on something for my new channel, time to do some heavy duty heartache cure research.

There's a lot of stuff out there. I find old wives tales about eating powdered willow bark and standing on your head. I find anecdotal support for journaling and talking to friends and cats (which, when put to the test, apparently works almost as well as just letting time pass). I find stories of people performing rituals involving burning mementos and photos, and there's more than a little advice on traveling, quilt-making, and pondering the quantities of marine life in the sea.

None of it, however, is very useful. It's just the inane babble of unscientific minds trying to make sense of their crumbling worlds.

But I'm in this to find an actual cure, a real solution. Something that'll work for anybody at any time. I'm not just trying to fill my time giving made-up advice so I don't have to think about my own life.

So my search continues. I take it in a more medical direction, and, after a couple of false starts and dead ends, I do find some sites that pique my interest. They catalog certain neurochemicals and their effects on the brain. I get particularly interested in two compounds called dopamine and serotonin. I suspect they may be responsible for the way I'm feeling right now.

It's a few hours later that I look up from my screen for the first time. Even though I'm finally on the right track, I still want to do nothing more than to run out and discuss all this with Bailey. I'm sure he'd find it very interesting. I'm sure he'd have some cool little insights and clever remarks.

You know that I miss you too, right?' the SSJ in my head says.

No you don't.'

A little chuckle. *'Of course I do! How can you not know that?'*

'Well, for one thing, you haven't contacted me in forever.'

'I'm probably waiting for you to make the first move. After all, you didn't reply to any of my invitations. What's a guy to think?'

'Invitations to go out with you and your freak-eyed girlfriend.'

'Come on,' Bailey says, *'that was a long time ago. Chlo and I are probably broken up by now.'*

'It's only been a few weeks.'

I wonder why it seems so much longer.

'Dude,' SSJ says, *'just send me a message. You know you want to.'*

I turn off my tablet. *'You have no idea what you did to me,'* I tell Bailey.

'What did I do?'

'You woke me up, that's what you did! You woke me from my peaceful little slumber and now you're forcing me to go back to sleep!'

'What?'

'You didn't have *to make me fall in love with you. Why did you do that?'*

'Hey, you make me sound like such a creep. Maybe you just misunderstood me?'

'Misunderstood you? What about all that landing my plane on your building stuff? What about all the accidental touching? What about all the messages you sent me?'

'Oh, that.'

'Yeah, that. What was that all about?'

But SSJ doesn't answer.

It's possible that my mind has started imploding, that it has thrown in the towel and begun a slow meltdown.

I need to talk to someone, get this out of my head and into a conversation. But who do I talk to?

I don't want to spend any more time with my colleagues than I have to, nor do I want them to know this much about me. I can't talk to my mom, either, for obvious reasons. My so-called friends have been out of touch for so long I feel like I should re-introduce myself the next time we speak, so who does that leave?

There really isn't anyone.

I feel a cold worm of static slip down my spine as I realize what I'll have to do.

I'll have to go and find completely fresh, new people. People I don't even know exist yet.

A very scary thought.

In fact, I'm not even sure I know how to do this.

I think back to the last time I truly met anyone new. I suppose that would have been Bradly Cooper, unibrow-extraordinaire. I subdue shudder, not a good example. Before that, chloe. Also not a good example. Before that, well, SSJ Bailey.

This isn't getting me anywhere.

And, anyway, I'm not sure this is what I *want* to do. In fact, I'm pretty sure this is exactly the opposite of what I want to do. I've never enjoyed meeting new people, they're just strange and scary and unpredictable and judgmental and boring. But it seems I've backed myself into a corner. My brain is stuck and if I don't find someone myself, Mom's going to set up something for me. Short from having her abducted by aliens, there'll be no way of stopping her.

This is going to happen one way or another.

I start a new Keep entry and brainstorm the least painful ways of getting past next Friday. Obviously it isn't easy for someone like me to meet new people. Sure, bumping into people I've never met is entirely within the realm of possibility, but actually *meeting* them is a whole different story. Not only will I have to find a situation where it's not weird for me to start a conversation, I'll also have to find common ground with them very quickly or the conversation will die. And if I do somehow manage all that, then I'll still have to find a way to set up a repeat meeting without looking creepy.

How do *normal* people do this?

I stare at my empty Keep entry for a long time before I realize I know exactly what to do. I've known all along. The solution to my problem is so simple, so obvious, that I almost didn't see it. It's just that it's up there with the scariest things I've ever done.

YouTube script:

So here's the weirdest tip you'll ever get for lifting yourself out of an emotional slump: slip into something really chic, some cool black number you look great in, stride out of the house confidently, and go Visit a Funeral.

Yup, I actually said that. And as always, bear with me…

Obliviously it shouldn't be the funeral of someone you know and love, just find a random funeral, there's always one going on somewhere.

The fun thing about a random funeral is that it gives you a chance to mingle with people ~~who are not your mom~~ and you can look in the direction of the casket and say to yourself: hey, at least I'm not *that* guy!

Or even better, remind yourself: My time here is limited, it's going to be my turn up there some day, so what's the point of being scared to take a chance now and then? We all end up in the same place, the only difference between us is going to be the amount of fun and love we experience along the way.

[put up a clickable google-map location]

I have more tips like this. Many, many more. And I've decided to do something I've never done before. Something huge! I'm going to give you the chance to probe my brain in person. If you'd like to meet up, just head over to this address tomorrow at 5 p.m. ~~And you'd better take me up on this offer before I come to my senses and change my mind!~~

[sign off]

25

Make sure to keep busy or life will seem increasingly meaningless.

The problem with internet related meet-ups is that, on some level, they never actually feel real. As I stand in the doorway of the café, checking to see if I can spot my followers, to see if they're scary weirdoes or just regular weirdoes, the one thing that goes through my mind is how easily I could turn around now and walk away. Ho easily I could head back to my car and forget about this stupid plan.

Who was I kidding, anyway? There's no way I can go up to a group of strangers and sit with them, even if they think they already know and like me. It's just not possible. It's not in my genetic makeup.

And what's the worst that'll happen if I bail? I left the house, so Mom should be satisfied – I'll drive around for an hour or so to make it seem more legit – and my followers, well, I'll thank them in the comments section for the lovely time we had. The ones who actually showed up will simply assume they missed me somehow and that will be that.

It'll be fine I tell my social robot. It's not like standing anyone up. It's nothing at all like breaking an actual appointment.

No one will get hurt.

So I turn around slowly, still worried that the robot will take over, still hearing my heart beating in my ears. I take my first careful step back towards the door, back towards freedom. But then someone bumps into me and starts yelling in my face.

"OMG! It's you! You're Kayleigh!"

It's a twenty-something girl with way too much eye makeup and long, dirty-blond hair. She hugs me like she knows me and proceeds to drag me along with her, deeper into the café.

"Where are we sitting?" she asks. "Over this way?"

I struggle to get free but her grip is like a vice.

"Oh! Is it these people?"

We move past several tables while I try to recover from the shock of being shouted at and then kidnapped.

"Are you here for Kayleigh?" she asks different tables. "YouTube? Anyone?"

We receive a volley of blank stares and my face starts to burn.

"Hey," someone calls out to us. "Over here! Kayleigh! Come sit with us!"

It takes a while for my brain to get back into gear. I'm wedged securely in a booth with several women who've put a glass of Coke in my hands and haven't stopped talking at me since they captured me. It's been one long stream of comments and unanswered questions and here's what I've learned so far:

To my left sits Mandy, the girl who grabbed me. She's in her early twenty's and has got boys on the brain. Literally every other statement out of her mouth is about boys. And you can tell she only throws in the other statements to balance things out. Missing out on contact with the opposite gender has definitely made her the girl-equivalent of a hormonal fourteen-year-old boy, which is some weird, caged energy right there.

On my right sits Sanieka, who isn't ugly exactly, it's just that she thinks she's so much prettier than she really is. And that confuses people. She tries to get away with things that much prettier women don't even get away with, and then she's baffled by the results. It's a terrible affliction that I'm not sure I'm equipped to handle.

Next to Sanieka sits the last of our troupe: Anatova. She's an older woman from Russia with a thick accent and a hard face that tells you her life has mostly been about survival. Now she's reached that point where she just wants to have some fun and, well, she's rightfully aggressive about it. She's not exactly fat but she's built in that sturdy, old-world way that lets you know that women can and do beat up on their men.

"American men are such little baby-cats," she tells me. "They always complain that Anatova should be more soft and gentle. I tell them, Anatova is woman, not bar of soap! You want soft and gentle you buy nice bar of flower soap. You want real woman, you come to Anatova!"

"Yeah, it's really hard to find a good guy," Sanieka chimes in. "Someone who treats you right because he's a gentleman, not because he's too ugly to do better."

I nod, not sure what to say.

"You're a real lifesaver," Mandy says, "helping us out like this." She nods in the direction of the bar. "So, when are you going out there?"

I clear my throat and test my voice. "How do you mean, go out there?"

"You know..." She makes some vague gestures. "Out here."

I still don't get it.

"You know," Sanieka prods. "To give us our demo."

"What demo?"

Mandy glares at me. "You don't seriously expect us to pick up guys without a good demo?"

"Da!" Anatova says. "Don't throw us into deep end, Kayleigh. You have to show us with example."

"How about that guy?" Mandy points out someone across the bar who is very obviously a model and quite possibly an Olympic gold medallist. By his demeanor alone I'd say he's waiting for his agent to take him to a photo shoot that'll likely be followed by a cocaine fuelled orgy.

"Why don't you pick him up for us? Should be easy for you, right?"

The guy notices Mandy pointing in his not-so-general direction and shifts uncomfortably in his seat.

"See?" Anatova barks at me. "You need to show us how not to scare away baby-cat American males!"

I'm appalled. "That's not what we're here for," I tell them.

"Of course it is," they say in unison.

Mandy: "You're here to give us some hands-on experience, right?"

Sanieka: "Of course she is."

Anatova: "Da!"

As the full extent of their misconception becomes clear to me I shudder and wonder how I got myself into this mess. Why hadn't I seen this coming?

"Look," I tell them. "I just invited you here for a drink. So we could discuss ideas and strategies, give each other tips, that kind of thing."

"Discuss things?"

"Give tips?"

They glare at me.

"You could, you know, pick my brain," I say hopefully. "I'll tell you whatever I think about whatever you want to know more about."

Anatova crosses her arms and almost knocks over her beers (she ordered several). "You need to paint us picture," she says, "not tell us thousand words!"

I wonder ruefully what happened to all the smiles from a few minutes ago. Am I not the same Kayleigh I was before, when they still baselessly adored me?

"You've seen my videos," I stammer. "You know that's not what my channel is about."

This is statement is met with blank stares, and I suddenly know how my grade school teachers must've felt, explaining a simple concept to a sea of dazed looking kids.

"I'm not some kind of a pick-up artist," I explain. "I'm not here to show you how to pick up random guys."

"You're not?" Anatova looks genuinely surprised. She's clearly missed the point of every single one of my videos. Mandy doesn't look too thrilled, either, and Sanieka just looks annoyed.

"I wasn't teaching tricks and pickup lines, I was trying to explain how to get close to your true love. And as my true love isn't here, I won't be talking to any guys tonight. And I've re-branded my channel anyway, I'm pursuing a much higher goal now."

"Okay, fine," Mandy says. Her eyes dart around the café, hungry and desperate. "You have your principles and we respect that, blah-blah-

blah, so just think of this as a little play, okay? Just pretend that dude is your true love." She points out a guy who is very obviously having a drink with at least two of his girlfriends. "Just role-play with him for us."

I suddenly feel very lonely, more than I usually do sitting by myself.

"Even if I were inclined to do that," I tell her, "it just wouldn't be fair. Not to him, not to me, and not to his two girlfriends."

"Kayleigh's got a point," Sanieka says. "We can't make some random guy fall in love with her just because we want a demonstration. That wouldn't be right." She thinks it over. "There's only one solution here. We have to get Kayleigh's true love to come here so she can demonstrate on him."

Mandy is immediately enthused. "Yes!" she says, grabbing my cell. "Let's call him."

26

"No!" I blurt out. "Give my phone back!"

There's no way we're calling SSJ Bailey to invite him to café where a bunch of my weird, overexcited followers are waiting to experiment on him.

"Why not?"

"You're just not!"

Mandy looks crushed.

Meanwhile, my pretend Bailey pipes up again. *'Come on, Willow,'* he says. *'I gave you my number, obviously I wanted you to call me...'*

'I can't,' I tell him.

'Of course you can. Don't you want to hear my voice?'

'I do, very much.'

'So just call me, dummy!'

'It won't do any good. It'd just be awkward and painful.'

Bailey scoffs at this. *'You can't know that. I could be sitting by the phone right now, waiting for your call.'*

'You could be, yes. But you're not.'

The discussion between the girls becomes heated. I signal a waitress for more drinks, hoping to stave off a full-scale mutiny. Then I realize I wouldn't mind a bit of a mutiny. At least it would get the attention off of me.

"Oh, look!" I say, glancing in the direction of the model-slash-coke-fiend. "I can't believe that just happened."

"What?" Mandy strains to see what I'm looking at.

"Don't look over there now," I whisper, "but I that model just checked Mandy out."

"He did?"

The girls take turns trying to gaze at the guy inconspicuously. His evening is about to get so much worse.

"Yup," I say. "He turned and looked straight at you."

For a moment Mandy can't believe her ears, then a thick, syrupy wave of smugness washes over her. "'Course he checked me out," she says. "He knows where it's at. He knows quality when he sees it."

"You sure?" Anatova says. "I don't see him move. I look at him whole time, he don't move."

"Sure he did." I turn to Mandy. "When Anatova looked at that guy with the two girlfriends, the model looked right at you. Then he said something to the barkeep. They were smiling."

Mandy trembles with excitement. "Yeah," she says. "They both want a piece of this!"

"Nonsense," Sanieka says. "When Mandy went to order she stood right next to that guy and he didn't look at her once. He's clearly not interested."

"It's classic reverse-desirability," I say, making up a fake concept. "By ignoring him because she thought she didn't stand a chance, Mandy has inadvertently triggered his value-seeking response."

"I have?" Mandy hangs on my every word.

"Of course. His rejection filter was overruled by his desire to be desired. He can't deal with the idea of not being wanted by someone as easy as Mandy. It makes no sense to him. He has no option but to assume there's something really mysterious about her."

"Go, now!" Anatova barks at Mandy. "Don't waste valuable time. Go and get baby-cat American pretty boy!"

But Mandy suddenly looks nervous. "I probably *should* go talk to him," she says, "but what if I wait a little longer? Make myself even more desirable? You know, the illusion of scarcity and all that?"

"Oh no," I shake my head vigorously. "It doesn't work that way with reverse-desirability. You have at most two minutes before he decides he was wrong about you." I look at my watch. "Better get moving before he disappears from your future forever."

I know this sounds cruel, but this is what Mandy needs right now. She came here for support and a little push. She wants someone to nudge her into action and then watch over her. And that's exactly what we'll do.

"Go!"

Mandy is ejected from our booth and decides, for reasons only known to her, to approach the bar using a weird kind of flanking manoeuver. I've never seen anything quite like it.

The girls cheer her on quietly.

When Mandy finally reaches the bar she takes the stool next to the model and, for a long time, for a very, very long time, she doesn't do anything.

Anatova can't stand the suspense, she calls out, "Talk to baby-cat pretty boy damn it!"

Mandy flinches. She shoots us an angry look. But, under the threat of further embarrassing outbursts, she finally taps the model on the shoulder and says a few words to him.

Which he ignores.

Intensely.

In fact, he chooses that precise moment to get up and leave the bar.

The self-contained bastard!

I really hadn't expected that. I don't have much experience with guys in bars, but I'd thought he'd at least be polite enough to talk to her for a minute before making up a believable excuse and leaving.

Somehow I still managed to overestimate humanity.

Mortified, Mandy slinks back to our table, but I make damn sure we receive her like a war hero.

"She did it, guys!" I hoot. "She went out there and she owned it!"

The girls all cheer. Anatova offers Mandy a few of her beers and Sanieka puts her arms around her and pulls her in. "We're so proud of you!"

Mandy slips effortlessly into her new role, she spends the rest of the evening telling ever taller tales of her glorious encounter with the model. And we listen, rapt, after all, Mandy is the only one of us who's actually interacted with a male tonight.

It's several hours later that I finally head home, tired but proud. For all its rollercoaster-like properties, I think I handled this evening rather well. I don't often spend this much time in social situations so I was worried it'd prove too much for me. But I survived. I survived and I even managed to communicate in a way that was somewhat meaningful.

But now it's time to unwind. Shutdown all the mental apps needed for social interaction, switch off hosting mode, and go back to being Loner-Willow (my default state).

As I follow a series of streetlights back to my car the crisp night air runs through my jacket and starts removing the smell of smoke and stale beer.

"Wait, hold up!"

A scruffy man with grey stubble pops out of the shadows and blocks my path. I assume he's homeless and wonder if I should run or give him money. Or both. Or neither. But then I spot a look of distant recognition in his eyes and realize he must be another one of my followers.

"Sorry, dude," I tell him. "The meet-and-greet is over. You just missed it."

"No problem." He shoots me a thin smile that cracks his face into a thousand tiny lines. "I just wanted a quick chat."

"I completely understand," I say. "But it'll have to be next time I'm afraid. At which point you might try being on time."

I walk around him but he moves to block my path again. "I wanted to get you alone," he says. He blows on his fingers against the cold. "I've been waiting here for hours, who would've thought you'd last that long in a social situation?"

Which is a strange thing to say to someone you've never met.

"I'm sorry." I walk around him a second time. "I have to go."

"Please, Willow, won't you just give me a moment?"

I turn and stare back at the man.

The one time I didn't wonder if a face in the crowd was my dad's. The one time I didn't search for familiar features (as seen in old photographs and the mirror (during those precious few seconds before looking into my own eyes starts to feel weird and I have to look away)).

I take a breath and look for those features now. I look past the scruffiness, which might just be down to his oversized coat and the grey stubble, and I do spot something. Around the eyes. Around the mouth. There are distant echoes of a mischievous smile, vague signs of high cheekbones and smoldering intelligence.

Yes, this could be him.

This could be my dad.

"I'm so sorry to ambush you," he says, still giving me that sad smile. "I know it's not a nice thing to do, especially after such a long time, but, well, I didn't know what else to do."

All that's going through my head right now is how different he looks from how my little girl brain remembers him. In my head Dad never aged. He never grew wrinkly and grey, he never stopped towering over me.

I stare at the man in front of me. I always wondered what I'd do at this moment. How I'd feel. What I'd say. But, even with almost two decades to prepare, I still surprise myself with what I actually say next.

Video #84 by *Kayleigh256*. Views: 256

Comments:

DissonantMelody: (11:27 am) It's good you have you back, K! Wish I could join your little meet up. I live sooo close!! But I'm traveling right now so \i won't be there! Hope you have another meetup soon!

TimyLiz: (12:43 pm) What happened to this channel? It was so funny before with all that stuff about flirting with waiters in front of your bf and giving too many gifts, then there's no posts for ages, then she comes back with this sad funeral shit. It's not that funny and, no, I don't want to meet up with you!

Squincyforu: (12:45 pm) Told ya his channel sucks!!!!

SchmidtAbout: (1:53 pm) <u>Date Nigerian Spam-Millionaires here!!!!!!!!!</u>

WhatsCrck: (8:28 pm) Okay, question for any guys out there: what would you rather have? 1. a really fat wife who's very funny, or 2. a sexy wife with who you'd never laugh again?

Allof12: (8:44 pm) How about neither?

WhatsCrck: (6:53 pm) No, you HAVE to choose

Allof12: (6:54 pm) If I have to choose, I take the hot wife with no sense of humor.

Loveislost: (6:55 pm) Why?

Allof12: (6:56 pm) Obvious! You can laugh with your buddies but you can't fuck 'em

Loveislost: (6:56 pm) That is so Saaaad!

WhatsCrck: (7:18 pm) It's not sad, it's valid socio-economical research!

DissonantMelody: (7:27 pm) You probably meant 'with whom you'd never laugh again' and 'social' research...?

GaryT3X: (8:36 pm) What about a smoking-hot embalmer, would you date her?

Allof12: (9:21 pm) Impossible. There are no smoking-hot embalmers. Natural selection bred them out of our species.

MandyGirl26: (1:11 am) Just back from my first meetup with da infamous K!! She's amazing. the real deal. I just talked to a super model!! The guy was totally into me!

SunnyAllDay: (1:22 am) Amazing meetup! Thaks again. U have to do that again soon!!

AnnyT: (1:24 am) Da! Babycat males much less scared of me now. This is great!

27

Topics for research: *Love and other sources of dopamine…*

I've always wondered what I'd do when I finally met my dad. How I'd feel. What I'd say. But, even with almost two decades to prepare, I still surprise myself with what I actually say to him.

Which is nothing.

Not a single word.

It's not that I can't think of anything to say, it's just that there are so many things I need to say that my brain can't order them into coherent sentences. The task is too convoluted and complex. So, instead, it just gives up.

"What do you think, Willow?" He gives me a sad smile. "Do you have a hug left for your old man?"

But he doesn't move in. He stands at arms-length, waiting for me to make the first move.

The clouds continue to pack overhead and I feel the first drops of rain on my face. It's going to pour any minute.

"Well," I finally manage. "I guess this means you're not dead."

"Looks that way." He lets out a little chuckle, but there are no laugh lines around his eyes.

"So it was you in the comments, then."

"Guilty as charged."

I look away, down the street. The rain's starting to come down and should get to my car before I get soaked.

"Now what?"

Dad shrugs. The sadness returns to his eyes. I guess he hasn't thought this far ahead, which is good. It means that, at least on some level, he understands this shouldn't go well, that he can't just pop into my life and expect a hearty welcome back. (And, for all I know, that's not even what he wants.)

On the other hand, it wouldn't have killed him to prepare. He's the only one of us who knew this was coming, so he could've spent some time considering the two main possibilities.

"We could get a coffee," he ventures, still staring out at some distant point in the rain.

"I suppose we could."

"There's a nice place just down the road."

There always is.

There's a whole world of places down the road. It's what we've built

127

society on.

Dad looks back at me. "What do you say?"

There's a crackle of thunder. My clothes are definitely getting soaked. Time to move.

I guess a few minutes isn't that much to ask. It wouldn't put me out. It'd give me a chance to dry out before the long drive home.

"Sorry," I tell him. "Like I said before, you're a little late."

I walk around him, and this time I keep walking. It's easy, actually, I just put one foot in front of the other, brace myself against the cold, the rain, and keep going.

And not once I do strain to hear if maybe he's coming after me.

Nope.

Back in my car I watch the rain pour down the windshield. There's so much going on in my head, my brain is flooding with thoughts and feelings and annoying questions, and that's really not fair. I was just getting things stable again, just getting over yet another hurdle in the bumpy road that's Willow's Life. Then HE pops up. Swoops in out of nowhere and destroys any semblance of balance, any hope of a quiet, normal existence.

There's just too much happening right now.

Only a few days ago I had no dad and I was on the verge of starting an amazing new life with SSJ Bailey. Now it seems one has been traded for the other, Bailey's out and Dad is in, but I didn't get to choose. I had no say in any of it. The trade was made without my consent, and that's not right.

When do I get to decide?

When is it my turn?

I take my tablet from my backpack and boot it up. It's time to start on a new series of scripts. I have more than enough data and shouldn't keep my followers waiting.

Draft YouTube script:

How to get over your crush, part 1:
Understanding what you're dealing with.

The first thing you have to realize is that love isn't actually real. It's not a physical thing that you can touch, like a scar or a wound, it's not a concept you can infer by its effects on its surroundings, like being late or feeling unsafe, and it's not even an emotion, really. Love is just a story that your mind tells itself to give it a goal and keep it busy. The emotion you think you feel is just a cheap cocktail of other, real emotions.

When you feel lonely, or bored, or somewhat without purpose, your brain chooses someone moderately compatible and convinces you this is the love of your life. It's a natural defense mechanism. Something to keep you alive, keep you interested. It probably evolved over centuries. With bigger mammalian brains came the advent of self-awareness, which brought with it concepts like angst, depression, and the realization that life is inherently meaningless – just a series of annoying moments during which you have to keep feeding your body so it doesn't die (in order to allow it to die at a later time). Self-awareness helped us figure out that life is a zero-sum game that cannot be won. All you can do is suffer along the way, and, the better you are at staying alive, the longer you get to suffer. Not a very good proposition.

So nature had to balance things out and give us something to live for. It knew we wouldn't be interested in her main goal, which was simply propagating a meaningless species. But how do you create meaning out of things that are meaninglessness? You can't. That's the problem. But, luckily, you can create the *illusion* of meaning. The *illusion* of fate. The *illusion* of purpose. And you do this by creating a story, such as love, and attaching a strong emotion to it.

Sadly, there were only a few basic emotions to pick from at the time, and they were all tied in with survival. For our love story we thus evolved a seemingly new emotion, which was actually a clever cocktail of Relief and Optimism.

Originally Relief was induced after a narrow escape from something horrible, like a famine or a bear attack. It was needed to stop us throwing in the towel. Sure, you almost died a horribly painful death, but here's your prize: Relief. And doesn't that feel great? Doesn't it feel like it wasn't so bad after all? Don't you feel like you could do just about anything now?

And Optimism was needed to keep us from jumping off cliffs every time life seemed hopeless, which was probably most of the time. Another long winter with no food, but hey, you never know, right? Over the next hill we might find some shelter, some food. In fact, we could stumble right into Nirvana if we just keep walking on this cold snow long enough. You never know.

So you mix these two emotions together, crank up the total dosage, and, presto, you have something quite powerful. Something so powerful, in fact, that the self-aware brain starts thinking of fate and meaning and her One True Love. Because, how could this person not be The One, if I suddenly feel this great?

But for those of us working on our heartache cures, it's important to remind ourselves that the person we think we have all these profound feelings for is not some super human created especially for us. It's just another idiot like the rest. Just some random person our brains decided to focus on. We may think they are smart and funny and interesting, but the truth is, if we found those exact same traits in our overweight neighbor, we wouldn't even notice them.

Still not convinced? Here's a little test. Think about your last breakup. The last time you really pined away for someone. What did you actually miss the most? Did you really miss HIM? Or did you just miss making that cool little future happen, the one you'd secretly planned out in your head?

Did you miss the person or the story?

28

Your brain is your worst enemy!

When sleep finally comes, it is restless and punctuated by convoluted dreams. Work the next day isn't much better, and when I return home, I find a stranger sitting in my living room.

I can't tell you how upsetting this is.

She's about my age, I suppose, with dirty blond hair cut in bangs and dark blue eyes. She's wearing a cute floral print dress and a red jumper.

I'm not entirely sure what to do about her.

Mom's nowhere in sight but this person's sipping tea from one of her fine china cups – the set she only takes out on special occasions – so unless this person is part of a new breed of burglar who breaks in to make herself a relaxing drink, she appears to be mom-approved.

I hang my coat and linger in the hallway, weighing my options.

"If you're looking for your mom," the woman says, spotting me in the doorway, "she went out to get cakes."

I briefly consider pretending I didn't see or hear her and going about my business, but my social robot won't let me.

"Ah," I say, my throat exceptionally dry. "Cakes, good."

"Are you coming in?" She gestures at the couch. "There's more tea if you'd like some."

I step into the living room, more than a little weirded out at being invited into my own home by a stranger.

"So, I was pretty surprised when your mom asked me over," she goes on. "She said you wanted to talk to me?"

"She did?"

I have no idea what scheme Mom's hatching now. I can only hope she doesn't expect me to go on a date with this person.

"It's been a long time," the woman says.

"What has?"

She frowns. "Don't you remember me?"

I shrug. I'm not in the habit of remembering people I've never met. I check my watch and wonder how long I'll have to sit here before someone or something, rescues me.

"I'm Melissa," she says. "Melissa Moretti. You used to come over to my house all the time, we used to play with Tamagotchis."

Ah!

This is my preschool pall, Melissa, the one who lived down the street. She moved away when we were twelve and I never heard from her again.

"It *has* been a long time," I say, feeling a little more at ease now.

She nods, nipping at her tea. There's an awkward silence and I'm not entirely sure whose fault it is.

"So," I try. "How did Mom find you?"

"Phonebook? Google? I'm not sure."

"And you just dropped everything and traveled all the way here?"

Melissa gives me a look. "Why not? We only live two blocks apart, and I didn't have much going on."

"You only moved two blocks away? Seriously?"

"Yeah. One and a half if you don't count the park."

"Oh. Somehow I remember you moving very, very far."

Melissa shrugs. "I guess two blocks is a lot when you're a kid."

"I guess so."

The silence returns and we look past each other as we try to think of things to say. Melissa sips her tea quietly, and, whenever our eyes meet, we smile politely.

I wonder why Mom keeps springing these kinds of situations on me. My life is just fine the way it is without her meddlings. (Except, of course, for the bit where Bailey refuses to realize we belong together and the bit where no one really seems to get me and the bit where Dad refuses to be dead, or to at least offer a good excuse for being absent all these years, and the bit where–)

Melissa stares at me. I might've been frowning at my thoughts. "So," I say quickly, "how is your import/export business?"

She gives me another look. "My what?"

"Weren't you running some company in the Philippines or something?"

"Oh, that." She laughs. "My mom keeps telling people that. Honestly, I'm not sure if she just doesn't get it or if she's deliberately trying to make it sound like a big deal." She puts down her cup and shakes her head. "So a year ago I ordered a case of special wart-cream from Shanghai. It turned out I was allergic to one of the ingredients so I put it up for auction on eBay. Some lady in the UK bought it. I suppose that sort of qualifies as import/export, at least in mom-speak."

"Right."

"It's not exactly a full-time job or anything."

"So, what's your full-time job?"

"It's being unemployed, I guess. I've had some bad luck lately."

"Ah."

"Yeah." She shoots me a sad smile. "My unemployed boyfriend left me after I lost my job. And he took our dog. And most of our stuff."

"Well..." I say, but I'm not sure how to finish that sentence. I did put a lot of feeling into the 'well' part, so maybe it's still comforting to her.

"Yeah," she says thoughtfully, "I guess things can only get better from here, right?"

"Of course. It's… it's going to be great, you just wait and see."

I check my watch again. It seems Mom's getting the cakes from China.

"So," Melissa says, "is your Tamagotchi still alive?"

"What? No. I lost that thing decades ago."

"Me too… Well, I lost it for one afternoon, then I found it again."

"Ah."

"You want to see it?"

Before I can say no, Melissa takes it out of her pocket. It's pretty scuffed and worn, but damn it if the thing isn't still alive. How's that even possible? This girl must be the Frankenstein of defunct electronic toys.

"Didn't you have to change the batteries at some point? Wouldn't that kill it?"

"Oh, I changed the batteries many times," she says, "but they show you how to do it on YouTube. You can attach a backup pair in parallel using a shunt so the Tamagotchi doesn't lose power."

Yup, I was right. A Tamagotchi Frankenstein.

My cell buzzes and I almost jump. "Sorry," I say. "I just have to check something real quick."

"Go ahead," Melissa says. "I have to feed her anyway."

bailey: hey you!

I stare at my screen for a moment, deeply hating how happy I suddenly feel. I remind myself I shouldn't feel as if something cool is about to happen – because it's not. It's definitely not.

bailey: where r u?
me: right here, what's up?
bailey: not much, about to go to the gym
me: why? u look great the way u r
bailey: nah I don't. u know my motto: come for the skinny arms, stay for the personality ;)
me: well I like u the way u r
bailey: see? It's working, ur staying for the personality :P

Melissa tries to look at my cell. "Is it good news?"

I shrug. "It's really hard to tell."

"Why's that?"

"Because good news and bad news look so similar these days."

"Ah." She nods wisely. "I know how that is."

bailey: so… I haven't seen you in the store lately.

me: oh, I was just busy

bailey: you must be running low on brazils, right?

me: i might have to come by, not sure when tho

bailey: ogreat! It will be really good to see you again.

me: really?

bailey: of course!

me: okay, well, I'll see if I can clear my day

bailey: So chlo said we should double date satruday. Did I mention that already? I don't remembver

And that's the whole problem right there.

While I've been moping around, thinking about Bailey, wondering what to do next, he's been busy forgetting about me. I don't even think he's noticed we weren't talking. And I can't tell you how disheartening it is to know that he has no problem enjoying his Willow-less life. It's a sucker-punch to the ego to find out that someone who knows so much about you, who's seen such a large part of you, still doesn't miss you when you're gone.

Am I *that* forgettable?

I put my cell away because there's no way I can reply right now. It's just as well, because Bailey doesn't send me anything else.

Melissa and I chat away for another hour or so, then she returns home to feed her cats and I head up to my studio to start on a new script.

Draft YouTube script:

I ~~believe there are many different levels to being over someone. The most dangerous level is where you can get through an entire day without thinking about your crush, where you don't even feel as if something is actually even~~ miss ~~ing from your life, but then you'll suddenly get a call or a message from~~ you ~~r crush and find yourself trying hard not to slip back all the way to the beginning.~~

How to get over your crush, part 2:
Keeping that voice in your head under control.

The second thing to remember is that we all have little voices in our heads giving us unasked advice. (*Come on, take that last piece of chocolate, it's actually good for you. You don't have to get out of bed yet, turn over and take ten more minutes.*) It happens all day, every day, and without us really noticing. And one of these voices is especially active after a breakup. It'll talk about your crush incessantly. It'll show you mental pictures of things you did together, things you could be doing together, and things you'd planned to do together.

It does this, supposedly, because it likes making you miserable. It is secretly against you. It's your own, personal, live-in Nemesis, and it knows you can't pine away without it reminding you there is someone to pine away for. Think about it, when your mind is elsewhere, when you're busy doing other stuff, you don't actually feel all that miserable. You can completely forget that you were sad. But this is upsetting to your Nemesis-voice so it tries to make you love your crush even more, never mind that they never saw your true value, that they never went out of ~~her~~ their way to spend time with you, ~~or that they ran off with a girl with one light blue and one grey eye.~~ Your Nemesis-voice doesn't care about any of that.

It's almost as if nature is secretly stacking the deck against species survival, giving us one more hurdle so we can prove our worthiness.

But now that you're wise to this, now that you know you don't actually miss your crush unless your Nemesis-voice tells you to, you can start defending yourself. ~~Fortify your thoughts. Weaponized your emotions.~~ You can train yourself to cut your Nemesis-voice off. You can learn to recognize its speech patterns and silence it earlier and earlier in its tirade. Especially when it tries to convince you that life without your crush is meaningless. ~~Even if, for a short period, it feels as if that is very, very true.~~

29

There are over seven billion people on the planet, so that's seven billion people, give or take, who don't like me.

Mom drops a piece of toast on my plate and goes back to moving stuff around the kitchen counter.

I'd actually like to talk to her about dad, tell her he popped up out of nowhere and ambushed me. Ask her how that's even possible, after everything she's told me about him. But I'm not sure I'd get the truth, or that I could handle it if I did.

Mom stacks some pots, humming a little tune.

"So, I met Melissa last night."

Mom turns and gives me a smile. "Oh, I'm so glad you liked that."

"It was actually pretty upsetting."

"Upsetting?" Mom shakes her head. "You haven't had fun in such a long time that you're starting to confuse having fun with being upsetting. Be honest, Willow, at first you were a little shy, a little scared maybe, but then you got over it and you had a good time."

"I don't think I did."

"I can't believe she only moved two blocks away," Mom muses. "I thought it'd take me years to find her, but there she was, right under our noses. Isn't that great?"

"I'm really not sure. This could have far-reaching consequences. You're meddling with forces you don't understand. Maybe we're not supposed to re-connect, did you ever think about that?"

Mom isn't listening. "Now you can play together again," she says enthused.

"Really? Should I order a vintage Tamagotchi? Should I waste my evenings keeping it alive instead of working on my channel?"

Mom waves it away. "Don't be silly," she says. "You know what I mean. You and Melissa can get together and do whatever it is people your age do. Compare your pipe trenches, make collages, that kind of thing."

"I hope you're not referring to my YouTube charts as collages. There happens to be a great deal of science behind them. It's not just silly pictures, I use a sophisticated mix of psychology, wrapped inside reverse psychology, infused with deep insights into human nature."

"I know you do, honey," Mom says. "And now you can do all that with Melissa."

"It's not that simple," I say. "The fact that we were friends at twelve and now live close doesn't mean a thing. There's no reason to believe we'd have any more in common than any two random strangers. And I'll thank you to stop making play dates for me."

Mom's face suddenly slips into serious mode. "No, Willow, I will not. Not as long as you keep shutting out the world like this. You need help or you're going to end up alone!"

I get up from the breakfast table because I've suddenly realized that breakfast isn't real. It's just a virtual concept invented by cereal companies. It's nothing but evil marketing and I can do just fine without that.

I get my coat and leave the house.

Here's what Mom doesn't understand. There's a huge difference between being *alone* and being *lonely*.

Being alone can be a wonderful thing. It can be really enjoyable. Sure, there's no one around, but the people who are not around are simply elsewhere. At some point they'll return and, until that happens, you can go about your business undisturbed.

Being lonely, on the other hand, is a different animal. When you're lonely you are in absence of a very specific person. Someone you really want to be with. Someone you miss and may never see again. Being lonely sucks on all levels.

Being alone is when you read good books, eat great food, and create wonderful art.

Being lonely is when the radio won't stop playing songs that make you cry.

Being alone is when you can pick your nose and dance in the dark with impunity.

Being lonely is when every part of you hurts.

Being alone is a temporary state that grows shorter with every minute.

Being lonely goes on forever.

And the solution to being alone is simply waiting for it to resolve itself, while the solution to being lonely is… well…

Actually, that's a tough one.

That one might need a cure that humans haven't invented yet.

At work my day refused to improve. There's a stack of reports waiting for me on, I don't hear a thing from Bailey, and every other minute my mind nips off to think about Dad.

To make things worse, Gary and Dorothy-Jane decide to hold an hour-long discussion right outside my cubicle. Their voices, once I notice them, are impossible to tune out, grating at my brain as if it's a piece of soft cheese.

'Listen to these them,' the Bailey in my head says. *'They haven't said a single*

meaningful thing so far. They're just making noise to hear themselves talk.'

I ignore him.

'Isn't it amazing how some supervisors just seem to fail upwards through an organization? Well, at least you don't have to work in a nut store, you should see the weirdoes I have to deal with.'

This is just my Nemesis-voice trying to make me daydream of Bailey, and I won't fall for it. Not anymore. I quickly open up a new report. Still, the day continues its worrying decline.

Dave from Purchasing needs an update on a new account.

Ramira from the party planning commission wants to know who's up for a mud-run.

And Denwa from Legal wants me to help find her cat.

Her best idea so far has been to make flyers for us to put up on our cubicle walls (what?), and around our neighborhoods (why?), and, naturally, her flyers are these last-century stencils featuring faded black-and-white photos. Exactly the kind of thing all other (ex)cat owners are putting up over the city. She has no hope of standing out.

I toy with the idea of helping her turn her flyers into real eye-catchers by hand drawing them, very badly, and then adding some glitters, but I'm scared she won't get it and get angry with me.

By lunchtime I'm convinced this day is out to drive me insane so lock myself in my car with my tablet to do some uninterrupted heartache-cure research. I'm particularly interested in finding out more about dopamine responses.

'Come on,' SSJ says, *'you don't need a cure, Willow. We'll be together soon.'*

'No, we won't.'

'Of course we will. We're just in a lull at the moment, that's all this is. It's happened to all the great loves in history. We'll get back together, grow old, and tell our grandkids about this silly intermezzo, you'll see.'

I don't answer. I'm not going to give in to my Nemesis-voice and I'm certainly not going to imagine what it'd be like to grow old with SSJ Bailey.

Nope.

I continue reading about dopamine instead and I suddenly get an idea. I run it back a forth in my mind a few times, just to cover all the angles, consider all the pros and cons, then I take a deep breath and put my tablet aside.

I know what I have to do right now.

And I know I won't enjoy it.

YouTube script:

**How to get over your crush, part 3:
The science.**

Ever wondered why being in love feels so good?
It's because your body rewards you by flooding your brain with two neurotransmitters called dopamine and serotonin. These chemicals directly influence the pleasure centers of your brain. In fact, these are the same feel-good chemicals your body releases when you use certain illegal substances, the same chemicals that make people think they enjoy exercise. This stuff, dear followers, is very powerful.

But, smart as it is, the body immediately performs a clean-up action after a big dopamine rush. It uses a chemical called prolactin to flush out all that nasty happiness. Prolactin prevents overstimulation of the brain's pleasure centers. It stops you wanting food after you've eaten an entire cake and it stops you wanting to be intimate after you've been way too intimate already. In short, without prolactin we'd probably get stuck in a terminal indulgence cycle.

So far so good, right? Sadly, when you're coming off the dopamine high of a crush, the prolactin isn't all that helpful. The world already looks grey and empty, the prolactin just makes things worse. The fact that your system floods with prolactin after a break-up is basically a design flaw.

So what can we do with all this knowledge?
We can't very well order our brains to produce more dopamine and less prolactin, can we?
Actually, we can. The first thing we have to do is keep busy, keep our minds pre-occupied so our Nemesis Voices can't trick us into wallowing, ~~the second thing is to find a way to beat what is essentially a dopamine addiction. [I need to do more research here!!]~~

30

"Mind if I sit here?"

I don't actually hear myself say this, my heart beats way too loudly in my ears, but the guy I'm talking to looks up and shrugs, so I guess he heard.

"Sure," he says, a little baffled. "Be my guest."

I know what he's thinking. He's thinking, why doesn't this chick go and sit at one of the fifty empty tables? But I ignore this thought and drop down in the seat opposite him. And I do it quickly, before he spots how nervous and fidgety I am.

He looks me over for only a second before he says, "Drink smoke pets?"

"Sorry?" I try to find my voice among all the beating noises, but it isn't easy.

The guy rolls his eyes. "Drink smoke pets?"

"I'm not sure I know what that means."

I might've picked the wrong guy for my dopamine experiment. I wanted someone a little sad and lonely looking. A guy I could have a slight upper hand with to minimize the risk of me passing out. And this guy looked just safe enough. Bland face but clean nails. No stains on his clothes but dressed as if even his mom has given up on him ever having a social life. And, most importantly, seated at the edge of the food court so an emergency escape would be possible.

This guy definitely looked like the ideal starter project. Alas, it appears he's quite insane. I don't even want to know the kind of hardships you have to suffer before you start asking people if they enjoy drinking or smoking their pets.

"I've never tried," I say, carefully pushing my chair back while assessing his threat potential. "I'm sure, though, it's a very rewarding pastime if you're into that kind of thing."

The guy snorts. "I'm just saving you time here," he says. "I'm not interested in a relationship if you drink, smoke, or have pets. So, do you?"

"Ah." I feel a million tiny muscles I never knew I had relax. This guy might not be an ax-murderer after all. "I'm sorry," I tell him, "You got me all wrong. I wasn't actually hitting on you, I just wanted to talk—"

"Come on," he says. "Obviously you *are* hitting on me." He brushes his hand along his nose, the way a more elegant male might brush back his hair – so much for hygiene – and says, "Here's the deal. I've got pretty high standards. You look okay, nothing special but not too ugly either, but if you're a smoker, a drinker, or a pet owner, you're just wasting your time."

Okay. So this is a very different kind of crazy from what I was worried about.

"I–"

"Although drinking is not too bad, I guess," he says. "In moderation, of course. If you want to have a glass of wine at my uncle Jerry's party next week, that'll be okay. But if I have to drive you home after then that's going to be a problem, because I don't have a license."

"This is not– I'm not going to your uncle Jerry's party–"

"Just as well," he says. "We want to keep it exclusive. No offense, but I hardly know you."

"I swear I'm not hitting on you, I just thought it'd be nice to have a short conversa–"

"And I don't really care if you have pets, either," he continues, "as long as you're willing to get rid of them. I have all sorts of allergies you don't want to know about. If you get rid of all your vermin and clean out your apartment, and I do mean really clean it out, get rid of every single animal hair, then that'll be fine."

"You're not going to see the inside of my apartment–"

"Just as well," he says. "My place is probably nicer. And bigger. But you can't bring your pets. It's not even allowed anyway, building rules. And if you want more than the top two drawers in the bedroom then you'll have to buy a second wardrobe yourself. I'm not paying."

"Stop!" I say, exasperated, "I just wanted to talk, that's all."

"Fine," he says, not skipping a beat. "I'm pretty good at that. I'm a member of Toastmasters, actually. Have you heard of them? They teach you to talk in public. They'll probably ask me to teach a class soon, because I'm a natural. You can come along if you want. We have a meeting tonight."

"I'm not going anywhere with you, because I'm not trying to pick you up."

"You are," he says.

I shake my head. "Not in the slightest."

"Then you're a pretty weird chick," he says. "A hundred empty tables and you want to sit here, with me, at a table for two. If you're not picking me up, then what the hell are you doing?"

This isn't going well. In fact, the situation would have to improve dramatically before I could even describe it as 'going badly'.

This is disaster squared.

"Look," I say, "we're both people, right? We're both part of the human race. What's so weird about sitting with a stranger every once in a while and asking them how they're doing?"

"That's a load of crap," he says. "No woman ever sits with a strange man, just to ask him how he's doing! The world doesn't work that way."

I really wish I could run away. In fact, I specifically chose this guy at this table because of the excellent running away opportunities. Sadly, the social robot has re-engaged. It won't let me get up and risk people staring at me. It won't have strangers thinking I am being mean, or worse, that I've just been rejected by this sad looking guy that they'll assume I was hitting on.

I have no choice but to prove to this guy that my motives are platonic and experimental. That my motives are far from ulterior.

"Look," I say, "not every conversation has to be premeditated, does it?"

"I call bullshit," he says.

I start to perspire. My only hope here is to pass out. To get swallowed up by a dark mist and suddenly find myself at home, hours from now, wondering how I got there.

Yes, that sounds pretty good.

"You have problems, lady," the guy says. "There's something seriously wrong with you. In fact, I'm starting to think you shouldn't even come to uncle Jerry's party."

"I'm not going to that party," I mumble.

He shakes his head at this. "You know what? That kind of relationship just isn't going to work for me." He takes his tray and gets up. "I can do better than you. Way better."

He turns and walks away.

I take a deep breath and watch him go.

Slowly, my brain comes back into alignment. It's over. It's done. I'm actually free. The world suddenly looks much brighter. It's like cloud cover breaking and letting in warm, gentle sunlight.

I'm alone again!

Securely back in my comfort zone now, I take a few moments to go over the conversation. This wasn't what I'd hoped for. I wanted to induce a dopamine reaction by talking to a new guy. Nothing major, like when I talk to Bailey, just something small, a tiny little drop to help me kick the habit.

That didn't happen, not by a long shot, but maybe a heavy dose of relief isn't so bad, either. Whatever chemical causes relief is probably related to the dopamine family anyway.

So, in a way, I got what I came for.

I take a few minutes to make sure I'm myself again, make sure all of the lightheadedness and nausea has passed, then get out my tablet. Strange as it may seem, this encounter has given me an idea for a new post on the fairness and purpose of physical attraction.

YouTube script:

I believe the key to a great relationship is a good balance between physical and emotional attraction. You need both at sufficient levels. It's very easy to say that looks shouldn't really matter or that you can always turn to a friend if you really need good conversation, but that's doing the human organism a disservice. We're simply not built that way.

Think back to that really cute guy you desperately wanted to talk to, but then he opened his mouth and nothing but boring nonsense came out. It was an immediate turnoff. Of course it was, no amount of beauty can compensate for a lack of personality. Talking to him was like being alone, only it was less interesting.

So the reverse is probably also true. Rivers of personality won't make up for someone being the total opposite of your type. And starting a relationship with no physical attraction at all would be a bad beginning of a long journey.

[chart# picture of beach with rocks –use google images instead of crayons?]

A long-term relationship is like a rock in the surf. A giant stone on the beach of life. It's strong, dense, tall. But waves will crash into this rock relentlessly and, eventually, it'll start to wear down, microscopic bit by microscopic bit. It's unavoidable.

If you start out with a huge rock – with heaps of emotional and physical attraction – you'll still have a lot left standing after twenty years. But if you start out with a small pebble…

So ask yourself, is your rock big enough at the start? Are you heading into your relationship with enough attraction? ~~Or are you going to settle for someone with nothing more going for them than a pair of colored contacts and some stolen Powerpoint wakeup lines?~~

[sign off]

31

Tip: *Don't assume you're the only one chasing your crush. Right now he's secretly talking to a couple of different girls.*

I'm finishing up my script when I get a notification of a new comment on one of my channels. I check it out and realize it wasn't left on my current channel, but under my very first post on my very first channel. The channel I put up two years ago, using my real name.

This post has only ever received three hits and at least two of them are mine. In online terms it's less visible than a needle in a stack of needles in a warehouse filled with stacks of needles. The only way to find it would be to search for it by name, so who could possibly have done that, and why?

But before I get a chance to read the comment, a flock of disillusioned teenagers descends upon the next table and starts throwing fries at me.

I take a few precious moments out of my day to wonder why these types of things always happen to me. How do idiots the world over instinctively know I'm one of their targets? Is it some kind of hive-mind telepathy thing?

I can only assume it's one of the many ways the universe enjoys toying with me.

Before it can turn really ugly I pick up my stuff and head back to my car. As I walk through the mall I make sure not to wonder what SSJ Bailey is doing right now, which means I have to detour along the west wing so I don't pass the nut store. And I definitely make sure I don't wonder if SSJ is still together with chloe. That kind of thought doesn't need to run around my brain.

Back in my car, I can finally read the mysterious comment:

From: OldMan1963
Hey kid!

I know I ambushed you the other day and that wasn't right. You need time to think things over, I get that. You were always big on thinking. Even before you could walk, you'd crawl around the living room with this big, worried frown on your face. Your mom and I would speculate for hours what was going through your mind.

But it's been a few days now and maybe you've decided it wouldn't be the end of the world to meet up with your old man. If so, I'll be at the

Dog and Whistle in the old neighborhood around six tonight. You don't have to come, I won't hold it against you if you don't, but I'll be there, hoping.

- your dad

I drop my tablet on the back seat and start the car. My plan is to keep my mind fully preoccupied with driving, but traffic refuses to help me out, it's way too light today. I circumnavigate pensioners and housewives with ease, and, before I know it, ancient thoughts rise to the surface. They're like pieces of a giant jigsaw puzzle I could never finish because the box lid was missing. I never knew what the picture was supposed to look like.

Some of the puzzle-piece thoughts go like this: Maybe Dad was actually a secret agent. Not like in the movies, nothing crazy like that, but he could've had an administrative function with an agency that tracked people. Bad people. And maybe some of those bad people tried to follow him home one day, so he had to go into hiding. He was keeping us safe by staying away.

Other puzzle-piece thoughts go off in a completely different direction: All those letters and birthday cards Dad sent, they were intercepted by Mom. Angry about him leaving, she sabotaged our relationship. At some point Dad decided to stop calling too, mom would always tell him I was too busy to talk to him. It'd take almost two decades and a neighbor explaining the internet to him for my dad to get around these roadblocks.

And other puzzle-piece thoughts are really vague: I may never know the details surrounding his disappearance, but some terribly dark mystery is at the bottom of it all.

I pull into the lot at work and quickly push the puzzle thoughts away. I shouldn't have had them as a child and I certainly shouldn't be having them now.

If this keeps up I'll have to charge Dad rent for the parts of my brain he's been squatting in all these years.

When I finally get home Mom greets me at the door in curlers and a bathrobe. I subconsciously note that there's no hint of kilos of shredded letters and birthday cards about her.

There never is.

"What's wrong?" she asks.

"Nothing, why do you ask?"

Mom follows me into the hallway. "I can see something's wrong," she says. "Did something happen at work?"

"Work was work," I say, hanging my coat.

"Before work, then?"

I turn to look at her. She's not going to let this go. I might as well tell her, she'll find out eventually.

"I think I'm going to talk to Dad."

Mom doesn't say a word. She follows me into the living room and watches as I turn on the TV and settle in on the couch. After a few more deliberating moments she asks me only a single question; "Do you really think that's a good idea, Willow?"

"Of course I don't," I tell her. "It's a terrible idea. It's probably the worst idea I've had in years. Decades even. But I think I'm going to do it anyway."

Mom considers this a moment, then gives me an almost invisible nod.

"Okay," she says. "Then that's what you'll do."

32

The Dog and Whistle is what you'd get if an American diner violated a British pub and its offspring was raised by Hungarians. From the high-quality upholstery to the cheap, laminated picture menus, the place is wrought with internal contradiction and crimes against style and taste.

As I enter I remind myself that Dad might not show. Or if he does, he's likely to be a few decades late – there's good precedent for that. Even so, I make a quick round before finding a table. (There are few things as silly as two people waiting for each other at opposite sides of a diner.) And, indeed, I spot Dad at the fifth booth in, sitting with his back to the door.

Again I have that thought: I can still turn and leave. I can still walk away and pretend I never made this particular mistake.

I can still make this never have happened.

But somehow I don't. Somehow I force myself to walk all the way to the booth and sit down. It almost doesn't even feel real. As if I'm watching some other daughter sit down with some other father for some other long overdue conversation.

I can't help but wonder how they'll do.

It doesn't help that this whole thing reminds me of the nightmare I had about Dad a couple of nights ago.

As I sit, Dad looks up and his face cracks into an uneasy smile. "Willow," he says. "You came."

"Seems like it."

"I'm glad you did."

He signals the waitress to bring me something to drink and I look him over. He looks different from the other night but also the same. It's as if I'm seeing him for the first time in years all over again. I try to reconcile his face with overused memories and old photographs, then I look for similarities with the face I see in the mirror every morning. I decide his is wider, with a nose that's more pronounced, but our eyes are the same. Or similar, at least. His are surrounded by skin that has millions of fine lines crisscrossing it that make me think of parchment.

My cell buzzes.

I ignore it.

"I'm only here to find out a few things," I tell him. "Then I'll be on my way."

My voice sounds thin and delicate. I hate that.

"It's okay, Willow," Dad says. "I'm just happy you're here." He reaches out to touch me, then thinks better of it. "Stay however short or long you feel comfortable with."

"I will."

Just looking at him I already know one thing I didn't before. All those times I caught someone's gaze in the crowd and wondered *'Are you him? Are you my dad?'* It never was. Not once. I haven't seen this man since he left.

I take a moment to compose myself, then say, "I hope you'll give me some straight answers."

"Of course. Anything you want."

Then let's just start with the big question, shall we?

"Why did you walk out on us?"

Dad looks wounded. "You don't exactly mince words, do you," he says. "I don't suppose you'd like to start with something a little lighter? Like, how are you doing? What have you been up to? That kind of thing?"

I shake my head. "Not really, no."

We've wasted almost two decades, this is not the time to drag things out.

"I guess not." He shoots me a sad smile. "You were always a determined kid. Very focused."

"I suppose I was."

"Right, I guess that means we'll just jump right in." He picks up his coffee and takes a sip. "It's not what you think," he says after a moment. "I didn't just get up one morning and walk out. That's not what happened."

"And yet Mom and I have been living alone for almost twenty years."

Dad nods thoughtfully. "I'm not sure what your mom told you," he says, "but it was a long and painful process. After everything that happened, and all the ways we tried to deal with it, it eventually became clear that we'd never make it work with who we were at that time."

I glare at him. "Could you be a little more vague, please?"

"I'm sorry," he says. "I just don't know how... Let me try this another way. I've always believed that, in any given situation, you should do the best you can. You should always try to find a solution that fits everyone best."

I shrug.

"But sometimes," he says, "after a lot of soul-searching, after a lot of failed attempts, you realize that there is no single solution that fits every one. Maybe there isn't even a solution that fits *any*one. Sometimes all we are left with is taking the least bad option."

I look out the window. Life is so much simpler out there. The people passing by the window, they all have easier lives than I do. The world is much nicer to them.

I swallow. I suddenly have this weird sense of déjà vu.

"And sometimes," Dad goes on, "you realize that the reason you can't find the answer is because the least bad option is one that doesn't include you. It's staring you in the face but you can't see it because you're not a part of it."

"Even if that made any sense," I say, "and even if I understood a fraction of what you think you've just said, you were still my dad, okay? You didn't have to leave *me*. You could've just left Mom. What did I ever do to you?"

I'm ready to get up.

I'm ready to throw in the towel and leave because I realize I didn't come here for answers as much as I came here to have my say. And I've just said all I needed to say.

Dad clears his throat and picks up his coffee. I instantly flash back to the heartless dad from my nightmare. The one who didn't think I was a real person. The one who allowed me to get stuck in sidewalk gum. But I know that this dad, the one in front of me, is different from nightmare-dad in at least in one way. The hand that holds his cup, it trembles ever so slightly. This man is not unaffected by our meeting. Not at all. There's a lot going on inside him.

I decide I can stay a few more minutes.

"Willow," Dad says, holding his cup with two hands as he puts it down. "The man who walked out on you and your mom was broken. He was nothing but a collection of shards." He glances up at me. The smile is gone, all that's left is the sadness. "I didn't know if I could be fixed and I didn't know how long it would take."

My cell buzzes urgently in my pocket but I ignore it.

"I still don't know what that means."

He tries again. "I couldn't allow my brokenness to break you two as well. A dad should be…" His voice catches. "A dad should be a rock, a protector, someone to run to for help. A dad doesn't deserve to be a dad if he's going to drag his family down with him."

My anger is starting to dissipate, and that really pisses me off.

I think maybe I started this conversation off still angry at the dad in my head and the dad in my dream. That man just seemed so cold and distant. But this guy is different. He's not better, necessarily, he still walked out on us, he never did call, but, well, he seems less deliberately guilty.

This man is just… helpless.

"I wanted to do whatever was best for you," he says. "If you only believe one thing I ever tell you, Willow, then believe that leaving you was the hardest thing I ever did."

I take a deep breath.

We look in different directions at nothing.

"So then why leave at all?" I whisper.

Dad looks back at me, but he looks at me differently now. It's as if he's searching for something, looking for clues. "You really don't know?"

"Know what?"

"You don't remember the accident?"

33

The things that really don't matter take up 90% of our time.

The waitress still hasn't come over. For some reason she keeps milling around the front of the diner where people have way too much food and drink already. She needs to get her ass over here so I can tell her about the AC. It's clearly broken, the temperature is dropping rapidly here.

Dad waits for me to look back at him, then says, "In your mind, Willow, when did I leave?"

I shrug. "A long time ago. I was little, maybe ten."

"You just had your birthday. Do you remember that birthday?"

My cell buzzes again. Somebody is desperately trying to get a hold of me. "Maybe," I say, wondering if I should pick up. "I'm not sure. I think I just remember that birthday from photographs."

Dad keeps pushing. "Was it a happy birthday?"

"What?"

"Were people smiling? Laughing? Having a good time?"

"I don't know, probably."

I think back and realize I only remember it from a *single* photograph. The one I found at the bottom of the old shoebox the other day. It shows our extended family gathered together at the deep end of our backyard, crowded together to fit into the shot. It's the only picture I've ever found of that day.

Was anybody smiling in that picture? Or were they just standing there, wanting to prove they'd been present?

I've imprinted the photo on my mind over the years but I've never really looked at it, not in that way. I think back now and realize there wasn't a single smile. All of us were staring into oblivion.

That must be why the photo always looked so eerie to me.

A bunch of dead, staring faces at a birthday party.

"Willow," Dad says. "What happened just before I left?"

"I don't know," I say immediately. I really have no idea, and if I did, if I had even the slightest notion, then I probably wouldn't want to talk about it anyway. There's no point in going to places like that with my mind.

"Think back," Dad urges.

It's really starting to freeze in here. Why isn't anybody banging away on the AC right now?

"Please, Willow."

"No." I slide out of the booth. "I hadn't planned on staying this long.

I'm late, I don't have time to listen to this nonsense."

Dad reaches out to stop me but I stumble back, out of reach.

"Willow, please…"

"I can't–"

"I know it's terrible what happened," he says, holding me in place with his gaze. "To you, to me, to all of us. Something like that shouldn't happen to anybody, ever. But we can't change how we got here, we can only choose how we move forward from here–"

"I have to go." I drop my gaze so I can step away. "I just don't have time, sorry."

A few more steps and then I turn and run. Through the diner and out into the street. It's the only way to stop Dad talking at me.

Back in my car I quickly take out my cell and nudge it to life, hoping to find a string of messages to keep me busy for a while. I can't imagine who was making the thing buzz so angrily. My dad was with me the whole time, my mom wouldn't know how to make it buzz, and Bailey hasn't made it buzz for me in a long time.

I try to pull down the notification menu but my fingers are trembling too much. The menu keeps popping back up. I stop for a moment and push back hard on whatever thoughts Dad was trying to stir up. It takes a good while, a full minute maybe, but eventually I'm calm enough to get to my notifications.

There are seven messages.

All from Anatova.

The girls are in trouble and I have to come immediately.

It's not that I *want* to see my followers, it's more that I want to *not* see them even less.

I have to keep busy and meeting up with them could go a long way. It'd be like going to a funeral, or to a sad movie, or standing outside a hospital watching sick people go in: a good reminder that, however bad life gets, there are always people worse off. Meeting up with my followers will be like doing some mental slumming.

I check out the coordinates Anatova has sent me but they're in a weird, numbery format. After some prodding Google tells me this is 'raw GPS data', actual satellite stuff. Luckily Maps has no problem with it and soon I'm on my way, driving across town.

Maybe this won't be so bad, I tell myself. I might even enjoy some part of it – the part where I get to talk to people who don't know the real me, who can't raise the really painful topics, or ask the really annoying questions.

At the very least I won't have time to think about Dad or SSJ. In fact, I should probably congratulate myself on not having thought about SSJ in a while. For days, actually. (Apart, of course, from occasional moments like this where I stop to congratulate myself on not thinking about him.)

Maps guides me to a mall on the other side of town where I find a parking spot close to the south entrance. I rush inside, following the coordinates to the back of the mall. There the trail stops.

I've reached my destination.

I look around. I'm in a food-court surrounded by cafés, ice cream parlors, and fast food places. There are a few people milling about but it doesn't take me long to determine the girls aren't here.

They've tricked me.

Or they've moved on.

I send Anatova an angry message asking her where they are. The reply comes almost immediately.

YouTube script:

How to get over your crush, part 4:
Other sources of dopamine.

Talking to other men (or women) will give you small doses of dopamine. Little drops of a neurotransmitter that initiates happy feelings. It won't be anything like what you get when you spend time with your crush, but we're trying to kick our dopamine habit here, not fuel it. Small doses is exactly what we need. ~~So find a sufficiently normal-looking guy at the mall and just ask him how he's doing.~~

In the not too distant future there'll be an affordable medical treatment for heartache. It'll be a matter of weaning you off the dopamine with a pill or a crème that sets your system back on a stable dopamine cycle, one without crazy crush-induced spikes. And this pill will also help curb that flush of prolactin that takes all the color out of the world when you get dumped. In the meantime, though, we'll have to find our own dopamine.

Natural dopamine is released whenever you do something pleasurable, so go out and do things you love. Not just things that enjoy, but things you really *love*! Go para-glide-jump-sailing. Buy another pair of shoes. Visit a weird country where the sky is impossibly blue and they mainly eat insects. You have some leeway to indulge yourself here because it's the lesser of two evils. ~~There might even be some danger to not getting over your crush fast enough. A prolonged unstable prolactin cycle could cause neurological damage. Damage you might never fully recover from, so get busy with the healing!~~
At the same time, try to stay away from objects, places, and activities that remind you of your crush. These kinds of reminders can give your Nemesis-voice a much stronger position of attack!

34

Anatova: right behind you!

I turn but I still don't see them. Not right away, that is. Then I realize the girls are actually in hiding. In fact, not only have they taken cover behind a series of potted plants, they're also dressed in black from head to toe and have elaborate utility belts hanging around their waists. Anatova even holds a pair of expensive looking night vision goggles.

These girls are deep undercover.

Although I can't say they don't stand out.

For the second time today I curse myself for planning out my day badly. This time I actually turn to walk away, though. Sadly, I don't get far. Mandy scoots out of from behind her plant, grabs me, and drags me back with her.

I'd fight her but that'd look even weirder.

"What the hell are you guys doing?"

Sanieka gestures frantically for me to crouch down behind one of the plants. "Anatova," she hisses, "debrief her!"

Anatova huffs. "Nyet," she says. "Not possible. Maybe you mean, *brief* her?"

"What?"

Anatova shrugs her large, meaty shoulders. "Debrief you do after mission. Brief you do before mission."

Sanieka frowns at her. "You sure?"

"Da, very sure."

"Okay, fine. So brief her already."

Anatova turns to me and gives me a serious look. "Here is deal," she says. "We have group of American baby-cat males cornered at frozen yogurt place. We follow them all day, collecting intel."

"Yup," Mandy chimes in. "They've been to the bookstore, the game shop, that electronic gizmo place, and they threw some coins into the fountain." She thinks for a moment. "Our intel suggests it was approximately one dollar and twenty-seven cents."

"Da," Anatova says. "They also spend time on mobile devices but we haven't been able to hack yet."

"Hack?"

Anatova waves it away. "There are ways, it's not difficult with right contacts." She hands me the night vision goggles. "We are now ready to strike. But here we need your help."

"We have the intel," Mandy says, "but we don't really know how to, you know, strike." She urges me to lift the goggles to my face. "It's the group of guys sitting at that table over there. See them?"

I refuse to use the goggles but I nod to indicate I've spotted them.

Mandy shoots me a lopsided smile. "Aren't they dreamy?"

Sanieka crouches closer. "Anatova knows a lot about this surveillance stuff, but we're not really sure how to use the data we've gathered."

Anatova gives me a sad nod. "Da. In past life they teach me to observe targets and silently decommission them. They never teach me to observe targets and then make them giggle and give me call for dance on Friday."

Mandy glares at her. "Make them giggle? Seriously?"

Anatova shrugs her big shoulders again. "They are American baby-cat males, they giggle. Deal with it."

"Whatever." Mandy turns back to me. "You have to help us make contact." Her eyes dart around the food court, perhaps scanning for mall security, approaching pre-existing girlfriends, or enemy aircraft. "What do you think," she says, looking back at me. "Can you do that?"

"Look," I say, "you guys are making this way too difficult. You don't need any intel or cold-war strategies. All you need to do is relax. Those guys will either like you or not. If they don't, you move on. It's no big deal."

I surprise even myself with that answer.

"Good," Anatova says. "Good. That's exactly what we need." She takes some dehydrated food from her utility belt and breaks it into four pieces. "Teach us how to relax, right now!"

"Yeah," Mandy says. "That's a great idea. Teach us how to stay calm around those dreamy guys."

Anatova offers each of us a piece of dried food but we all decline.

"Well," I say, "I guess you just decide to stop worrying."

"We don't need guesses," Anatova barks. "We need to know how to relax for sure!" She fidgets with her belt, running a nervous finger over what I hope is not a smoke grenade.

"Okay, okay," I say. "One way to go about this would be to just walk up to them and start a conversation. How about that?"

Sanieka and Mandy share a look, information passes between them silently, then Mandy gives me a nod. "Yes," she says. "That's so crazy it might actually work."

Anatova agrees. "Da. Very good. Targets will not see that coming. This is what we will do."

She chews some of the dehydrated food and puts the rest back into her belt. Then, for a very long time, nothing happens.

"So," I prod. "Are you guys going over there or not?"

Another look passes between them and they seem to come to a unanimous decision. "We're not," Sanieka announces. She grabs my arm, Mandy grabs the other, and they push me out of hiding.

"Hey guys!" Mandy yells, ducking back behind the plants. "This girl wants to ask you a question!"

The dreamy guys look my way.

I'm caught in the headlights.

"Oh, yeah?" One of the guys says. "What's that?"

My heart starts to race, drowning out all other sound, and the world suddenly seems to be sloped at an angle, but, somehow, I manage to start moving.

The first few steps are horrible. They actually hurt me physically. The only thing that even keeps me going is the knowledge that doing anything else would be even more embarrassing. The guys have already seen me, so there's no way back.

The steps in the middle aren't actually that bad. They're no fun, but I don't actually have to do much, just keep myself upright and moving forward, and I can do that, I've been practicing since birth.

But the last few steps, the ones just before I reach their table, are pretty bad again. They're bad because I know that soon I'll have to stop walking and start doing something else. Like talking. To guys. That I don't know.

I hazard a quick look over my shoulder but Mandy, Anatova, and Sanieka haven't moved. They're not coming with me. When I look back I'm shocked to see I've already reached the table already.

It's time to stop walking and start talking.

Video #97 by *Kayleigh256.* **Views: 271**

Comments:

Squincyforu: (9:28 am) This channel gets funnier every day! This gril is hilarious!

SoundAvice: (1:10 pm) R u kidding me? You know she's dead serious about this stuff, right? This is her actual advice. She really thinks she's helping people!

Motiva8: (2:22 pm) <u>Make your timeshares larger here!!!!!!!!!</u>

OldMan1963: (3:42 pm) Are you there, Willow? I know that was a little rough but we got through it, didn't we?

LoveIsLost: (3:42 pm) K. your new stuff is even better! Even if I don't really understand it all yet, I know it's good. Keep paving the way for us!

OldMan1963: (3:44 pm) We can take this however slow you want but, please, let's stay in touch.

AuntieA: (3:44 pm) Auntie looking for her Nigerian prince. Where did you go?

Squincyforu: (3:51 pm) Thumbsdown on tis one. If this is really meant to beserious, and it seems os because you don't respond to the accusations, then shame on you!

OldMan1963: (4:42 pm) Please, Willow, talk to me. I can't lose my little girl a second time...

35

I stare at the guys while my mind runs itself ragged trying to remember my video posts. I know what to do, don't I? I've been vlogging about this kind of thing for ages, I just have to remember one little piece of my own advice. Just one.

"So," one of them says, a tall guy with unruly, dark hair, "what's the question you wanted to ask?"

"Well–," I stammer, trying to buy some time. "I just need to know, by show of hands if possible, how many of you, erm, pee in the shower."

They stare at me.

I try to keep my voice steady as I push on, holding up my cell in a trembling hand. "I'm doing a survey, so no lying please."

The guys look at each other, then burst out laughing.

"Definitely Joe," one of them says.

"What? Why me?" the tall, dark one says.

"Are you saying you don't?"

"Yeah," I chime in. "Are you some kind of prude? There's water all around you, are you really going to step out of the shower, get the whole bathroom floor wet, just to go to the toilet? What's wrong with you?"

"Yeah, man," one of the other guys says. "Who does that?" This guy is older, late forties, early fifties. He might be the dad or uncle or colleague of one of these guys. His hair has a reddish tint to it and there are some freckles above his brow. I turn on him in a flash. "So you *do* pee in the shower?" I roll my eyes at him. "I knew it. You think the whole world is your own private toilet, don't you!"

"Hey!" he says. "That's not fair! You just called Joe out for *not* doing it!"

"Who said anything about being fair," I say. "This is just a survey. Privately I think you're all degenerate perverts."

They laugh again.

For all my nerves I notice I'm starting to enjoy myself a little.

"So I have one for and one against," I pretend to type something on my cell. "What about the other two?"

I notice that my demeanor's changed also. I threw out that first line more or less in a panic, trying to break what would otherwise become a very awkward silence, but that last line came out sounding a little chipper and upbeat, you know, the way a real girl would've said it. One of those fun chicks who doesn't care what the world thinks about her.

How did I do that?

"Damned if I do and damned if I don't," one of the remaining guys says. He's shorter than the others, has a sizable beard, and a bit of a potbelly. It suits him.

"Might as well come clean if you're damned," I point out. "So, which is it? To pee or not to pee?"

"I'm going to go with… sometimes?"

I tsk. "Sometimes? What does that mean?"

"It means I try to go *before* I hit the shower. So, no water on the bathroom floor and no pee in the drain. Perfect."

"And no fun in the bedroom," I retort, shocking myself.

The others burst out laughing. I suddenly realize part of what's happening here must be context. I'm not trying to hit on these guys, I don't even need them to like me. I'm just here for my girls. Doing an intro for them. Any rejection I suffer won't even count because I'm not actively interested in any of these men.

Yup, it's much easier to approach people on someone else's behalf.

I look over my shoulder and see that the girls have finally left the safety of their potted plants. Sanieka and Mandy approach carefully, still looking a little skittish, while Anatova veers off to the side, making some kind of flanking maneuver, possibly trying to keep the sun in her enemy's eyes as she comes in low from the west.

"So," I tell to the guys, "I'm about to introduce you to a couple of very interesting girls."

"Really?" They glance around. "Where are they?"

"They appear to be flanking at the moment, it's hard to say, but they'll definitely be here soon."

"It's not those weird chicks with the binoculars who were following us, is it?"

"Yeah, I think I saw one of them counting the change we threw in the fountain."

"I wouldn't know anything about that," I say quickly. "I just know these girls pretty special."

Mandy arrives first. She takes up position next to me and gives the table a forced smile. She's all nerves.

"This is Mandy," I tell them. I'm about to expound on her background and interests, but realize I don't know the first thing about her. I decide to go rogue, instead. "Mandy is a total freak."

Mandy gasps.

"You wouldn't believe the things she gets up to."

The guys don't seem to mind this description. If anything, they look at her with renewed interest."

"Does she pee in the shower or the toilet?" Joe wants to know.

Mandy looks at me in horror.

"Dude," I tell him. "My girl here doesn't even *own* a toilet."

Mandy shoots daggers at me with her eyes. "Don't worry," I whisper.

"It's just a running joke, you're fine."

Sanieka arrives and I intro her to the table as well. Anatova is close behind, pushing out her chest as she announces, "I am here!"

The guys look her over, curious to see what she'll say next, but she adds nothing. She merely smiles mysteriously.

I've taught her well.

"I can't tell you anything about Anatova," I say to the guys. "It's all highly classified. Maybe, if you're lucky, she'll tell you something about herself, but whatever she says will either be a total lie or a very dangerous fact."

The guys seem mildly intrigued, and that's not a bad start. I'll take it. They introduce themselves, besides a Joe, there's a Harry (the older redhead), a Jean (the potbelly guy), and a Tom (the invisible one – if this were a movie, he'd be killed in the first act.) They pull us up some chairs and the girls and I soon fall into a groove, chatting away like pros. Whenever we're at a loss for words, or get a difficult question, we just smile mysteriously. This strategy works even better than I imagined it would when I made it up in my dark, empty studio weeks ago.

"That's an interesting belt," Harry says to Anatova at some point. He pulls some dehydrated food from one of the pockets and looks it over. It's hard to say whether his fascination with Anatova is the kind he reserves for potential mates, or for unexpectedly interestingly shaped roadkill, but either way, Anatova is ecstatic.

"Is highly efficient, no?"

"Sure. In fact, I should probably get one. I could keep fishing lures in there."

"This is YQ-23x utility belt!" Anatova barks. "Military grade! Is not for fishing toys!"

"Of course," Harry says, "but it could be, right?"

"Well, yes. Technically could be," Anatova concedes. "But is not."

"You should put a compact in there, Harry," Joe jokes. "Then you don't have to pretend to use your cell every time you want to check your hair."

"Hey!" Harry says. "If you had hair like mine you'd do that too."

"Mirror would be good," Anatova interjects. "Perhaps with telescopic handle, adjustable neck, rotating bezel. I think is good plan."

The conversations bubble on for about an hour with only the occasional silence. When the guys finally decide to take off, none of the girls has the presence of mind to ask for a number. I let it slide, though. I'm not convinced there's a The One for them in this bunch, so we'll just think of this as practice.

After a few more minutes I bid the girls goodbye, too. I have to get home. I have an idea for a script and I need to write it down or it's going to burst out of my brain some other way.

YouTube script:

Without wanting to sound dramatic, there really is a lot to get up for in the mornings.

I won't bore you with the obvious stuff. The gorgeous sunsets, the beautiful flowers, the people who 'probably' love you, blah, blah, blah. We appreciate all that, but it's not what gets us out of bed. We need more, because we know that life is inherently meaningless. That we've collectively decided to create a complex set of filters to help us ignore the fact that everything we think of as meaningful is just stuff we do to keep busy.

Do you think your job or your self-made company matters? Try shutting it down and see if anyone really notices. You think your hobbies and past times matter? Try not doing them for a while and see if the world ends. ~~You think your significant other matters? Try introducing him to a girl with weird contacts and see how fast he forgets you.~~

So why get up at all? ~~Especially if life seems more like a series of trials than a hot pocket of wonderful opportunities?~~

Well, we should get up because every time we manage to get out of bed we're presented with an entirely new day. A day on which anything can happen. Today doesn't know about all the horrible things that yesterday did to you. It's not going to just continue that pre-set course. Yesterday is fully in the past and any aspect of it can change for the better today. Nothing is set in stone.

And if nothing really matters in the long run anyway, then we also don't need to worry as much as we do. Our only real task is to find a way to get out there and enjoy ourselves.

[signoff]

36

Reminder: *Not a cool joke for the office: I'm going to the toilet, you guys need anything?*

The next morning I pull a random set of clothes from my closet and head down for breakfast. Mom's making toast. I take a plate and sit at the table.

"Sleep well?" she asks.

"I'm not sure," I say. "I wasn't consciously participating."

Mom slides a piece of toast onto my plate and returns to the toaster without making eye-contact. "So," she says over her shoulder, "how are you today?"

"I'm okay."

"How did your meet-up go?"

I take a moment to gather my thoughts. "Well," I say, "Dad wasn't dead, so that's one thing." I blow on my toast. "I guess it's fair to say your reports on that matter were greatly misleading."

"Did he look… okay?" Mom doesn't turn. "Healthy and everything?"

"I guess. He looked healthy enough."

"Good."

She doesn't sound nearly as casual as she thinks she does, there's a definite edge to her voice.

"He looked normal. You know, just a regular guy."

"Did he try to bring up anything… problematic?"

I pretend not to hear, but Mom presses on. "I mean, did he want to talk about the past?"

"The past?" I shuffle the toast around my plate. "Like Nero burning Rome and the eighty-year war? Not really. Somehow it didn't come up."

"You know what I mean," she says. "Did he say anything about what happened before?"

I'd really hoped this wouldn't come up.

"I don't want to talk about it."

"Neither do I," Mom sighs.

I look over at her and realize she's not doing anything. She's not actually mom-ing, she's just moving plates back and forth between two stacks on the counter.

"If neither of us wants to talk about it," I say, "then maybe we shouldn't."

She sighs again. This time it's not weariness, this time it sounds more like exhaustion. "I know it's hard," she says, "but maybe we *should* talk about it, don't you think?"

I don't. In fact, I suddenly feel very strongly that it's time for me to leave.

"Your dad and I could never agree on how to handle it," she says, her voice little more than a whisper now. "We had very different ideas on what to tell you and what not to."

"I don't have time for this," I warn her. "I'm late as it is."

"No." She clears her throat. "I think maybe… I think maybe I made a mistake, Willow. A big mistake–"

"You didn't," I cut her off. "Whatever you did, it was fine. I'm okay. Everything is okay. Let's just forget about this."

Mom shakes her head, still with her back to me. "I don't think we can," she says. "I thought we could go on like this, but it's just not working."

"It is. Everything is working just fine. Whatever you want to tell me, whatever it is, just don't. I'm fine with the way things are. Just let it be, okay?"

"But you're *not* fine," she says, her voice trembling. "And *I'm* not fine. And your father–"

"Stop it! He didn't say anything so we don't have to talk about this."

"He was right," Mom whispers. "I shouldn't have tried to shield you from this. I shouldn't have locked away our old stuff, our old photos…"

I glace at the kitchen door. It's so close. Just two medium-sized steps from the table. Why aren't I moving?

"I thought this way would be easier on you," she continues. "I thought…"

She still hasn't turned around. And that's a good thing, because I don't think I could stand her looking at me right now. Not with what she's saying.

"All I tried to do," she says, "was stop your pain. I couldn't stand to see what it was doing to you. So I did what I could to protect you. I never thought for a second it would end up hurting you more."

I send hurried commands to my non-moving legs: *Start walking! Now!*

"I'm so sorry," she whispers. "I really hope you know… I hope you understand… it wasn't your fault. None of it was your fault." She clears her throat. "It wasn't anybody's fault."

With heroic effort I finally get my robot body to move. Slowly at first, one step at a time, but then I start to pick up pace along the way. Mom keeps talking, I can't make her stop, but I can keep my mind busy while I drag myself from the kitchen. I can keep myself from absorbing whatever she's saying.

My struggle to keep my mind in check continues at work. It's difficult because something tries to drag my thoughts towards darkness. It's as if the more I try not to think about what Mom was saying, the more I do.

Thankfully, crazy Denwa from legal finds a way to distract me.

"Willow," she says, popping her annoying little head over my cubicle wall, "you'll never guess what happened! I found her!"

She looks insanely happy.

"Found whom?" I ask.

Denwa waves her cell at me by way of explanation. The screen shows a selfie of her holding a distraught looking pet.

"My cat! Can you imagine that?"

I tell her I'm not sure, I've never tried.

"I mean," she says, breathless, "how many times have you heard of a missing cat being found?"

I shrug. "Never?"

"Exactly!" she says. "It never happens!" She claps her hands excitedly – which I feel, even given the circumstances, is a bit much.

"That's great," I manage. "Please feel free to take your flyers back home with you." I point at my cubicle wall where she's stuck a generous number of her pleas for help.

"No problem!" Denwa beams. "Oh! Lenora! Have you heard the wonderful news?"

Lenora's vicarious excitement is so intense and so immediate that I worry she might faint. Luckily Denwa takes her away to share the great news with the rest of the department. Sadly, this means my cubicle wall remains helplessly marred by impromptu cat literature.

As soon as the girls are out of earshot, though, my dark thoughts return. My Nemesis-Voice demands I analyze what Mom and Dad were trying to dredge up. I do my best to fight it. I can't let my mind to go to that place.

I look up some old YouTube scripts on my hard drive and start reading, focusing intensely on my old thoughts and insights. I keep going until I reach the draft of my latest script, just to remind myself that, no matter what Mom and Dad tell me, there really is nothing wrong with my beautiful brain.

Draft YouTube script:

How to get over your crush, part 5:
Letting time pass.

[note to self: this is very obviously the main point. Eventually time heals all. It has a way of muting things and evening them out. But simply waiting for this to happen is not good enough. There must be a way to speed this up. Maybe even intensify it. Should look into this pronto!!!]

37

Mom finds a plethora of ways to avoid me the next couple of days.

It's nothing too obvious, nothing too creative, she just happens to be somewhere I'm not. When I come home she's working in the garden. When I watch TV she's in her room. When I make myself something to eat I find a note saying she's out with her knitting club.

I don't push it. I still need time to calm my brain down, let it know that it is fine, that it isn't in need of new, scary information. And I know Mom is brooding, anyway. She's cooking something up. Best to steer clear of her for the moment.

So the week continues more or less uneventfully until Friday, when I get another message from Dad. He wants to know if I've gotten used to the idea of seeing him yet. He wants to know if I'm free for lunch.

This is surprising because part of me expected him to disappear again. A rather large part, actually. I thought he might have satisfied whatever small amount of curiosity made him look me up in the first place and that would be that.

But here he is, still hanging around, still pushing to see me. I wonder why that is. Try as I might, I can't think of a single reason. It's almost as if he was telling the truth about not wanting to leave me in the first place. And I really don't know how I feel about that.

"Willow!" Dorothy-Jane grins at me over my cubicle wall. "What are you up to, girl?"

A social weight drops on my shoulders. I was hoping for some quiet time, some alone-with-my-brain time where I don't have to navigate any social pitfalls, but it seems my self-appointed office rival has chosen this precise moment to marshal her next attack.

Fine.

This is what we'll do then.

"Just a sec," I tell DJ.

I read back my reply to Dad, make sure it explains very clearly what I think of his plan to meet up again, then press send. (I really hope I'm not making a big mistake here.) After this, I turn back to Dorothy-Jane, who's still grinning at me patiently, and give her a broad smile. I'm sure she's found a crafty way of getting back at me for accidentally letting Gary know that the Krestmont report was actually mine. Let's find out what it is.

"What's on your mind, Dorothy-Jane," I say, surprised to hear I sound exasperated rather than scared. I didn't know I was going to do that, or that I even had it in me. "It's a bit early for you, isn't it? Aren't you supposed to be sleeping in as per usual?"

"Ouch," she says. "But you're right, I've been a little late these last few days."

"Actually, it makes perfect sense." I still sound impressively unscared. "After all, what's the point of coming in before I've done enough work for you to steal?"

What is going on with me? Have the last few weeks actually built me up – or broken me down – enough for me to start defending myself?

Dorothy-Jane's grin wavers. "Oh yeah, the Krestmont report. Sorry about that. Gary got it into his head that it was mine. I tried to set him straight but he steamrolled right over me. You know how he is."

"I guess…"

"I should've tried harder, I know, but, well, it didn't seem all that important. We're all on the same team anyway, right? As long as the reports are good, we all look good."

"Yet some better than others," I say.

She waves it away. "I wouldn't worry about it. Gary can't tell any of us apart, anyway. I can't tell you how many times he's mixed me up with Janine." She smiles conspiratorially. "To him, this whole department is just an amorphous mass of financial-problem-solving matter."

I nod carefully. Is this a trap? Why does it feel like she's being nice to me? "Either way," I say, trying to sidestep what I think is some elaborate kind of trap. "You probably didn't come in early just to apologize to me, so I won't keep you."

"Oh, I'm in no hurry," she says. "I just wanted to clock in early so I could leave before five." She gives me a wink. "I have a hot date!"

Ah. That's why she's here. She came over to rub her date in my face. "How nice for you."

"Yeah, I thought you'd want to know."

"Oh… Why?"

Dorothy-Jane winks at me again for some reason. "Don't worry," she says, "your secret is safe with me." She finally steps away from my cubicle wall. "I have to go practice my PowerPoint wake-up line in the lady's room," she says. She winks at me one more time, then disappears. It takes me a moment to process what's just happened, then I stare after her, unsure if I'm still supposed to fear her or not.

"How have you been holding up?"

Dad smiles encouragingly as I sit down.

Again I note how different he looks. I just can't get used to seeing him like this. The little girl in me still expects the man from the photographs, the one with the corny mustache and the big hair. The one who towered over her and made her feel safe.

I remind her that that man doesn't exist anymore.

I remind her that, no matter what happens today, no matter how she restructures her life from here on in, she'll never get back what she lost.

That little girl will never get her dad back.

"I didn't know if I was going to see you again," Dad says. He almost puts his hand on mine, but again stops short at the last second. "The way you walked out," he says, "I thought maybe I'd blown it."

I don't know what to say. There's no point in telling him how close we came to that being true.

The waitress comes by and I order some tea.

"So," Dad says, after she leaves, "does your mom know you're here?"

"She knows."

"And she is okay with us talking?"

"I wouldn't go that far."

"But she tolerates it?"

"I wouldn't go that far, either. Let's just say she's aware of the proceedings."

It's dangerous for me to be here, I realize that, but I couldn't stay away. This man is my father, after all. I don't want to be the reason we lose touch forever. That's so final. But I can't seem to make any first moves, either. He broke that part of me. As long as we don't talk about any dark subjects, though, I think I'm okay with seeing a little more of him.

"Well," he says, a careful smile forming on his lips. "I guess we'd better proceed, then."

38

The waitress passes our table and gives me a look as if she's trying to remember something, then she makes one of these 'Oh-yes!' faces and hurries away.

"So," Dad says, giving me a searching look. "You didn't answer my question. You were pretty upset last time, how have you been holding up?"

"I'm holding up as well as can be expected," I say. "Just battling the futility of existence on a day to day basis like the rest of humanity."

Dad chuckles as if I've made a joke. "That's my Willow," he says. "Always overthinking things, looking for deeper meaning." He gazes out the window and frowns, as if pulling a reluctant memory from a distant corner of his mind. "Even as a toddler," he says, "you had this strange, quirky way of looking at the world. Your thoughts always seemed so alien, so counter-intuitive. But then you'd explain them to us, this tiny girl holding miniature lectures in the living room for her parents, and suddenly it'd be impossible for us not to see the world through your eyes."

I shrug. "I suppose I have that effect on people."

I sound casual, I think, but inside there's a lot happening. Something warm starts to uncoil and I'm not sure I like it. It doesn't feel entirely like me.

"You do," Dad says. "And it goes a long way in explaining why they gave you your own TV channel."

"My own what?"

He searches for words. "You know," he says, "your dating show."

I cringe. "My channel is not a dating show, and it's not on TV. It's an internet research channel chronicling my exploits in charting the human condition."

"I'm sorry if I said that wrong," he says. "My neighbor explained it to me. He told me your channel is on every computer in the world."

"Well, that's one way of looking at it."

Dad gives me a serious look. "Don't sell yourself short, Willow. Please don't ever do that." He takes a breath. "I've been reading the comments from your followers, you're making a real difference in their lives. For many of them you're the only person willing to listen and guide them through difficult times."

I shrug. The waitress is taking forever to bring my tea. Perhaps she decided to hand-pick the leaves in rural China.

Dad clears his throat. "You turned out so well, Willow. I don't think I'll ever be able to express how proud I am."

I look around for another waitress, but there isn't one.

"I always was," he goes on, his voice thin. "I always knew you were special. I couldn't wait to see what you'd–"

His voice catches. He takes a sip of coffee and closes his eyes.

The waitress finally returns to our table and I thank her for the tea. I'd say something to Dad but I wouldn't know what, or even whether I have a voice at the moment.

He finally looks back at me. "That's why I couldn't risk my problems damaging you," he says. "I couldn't take the chance of you not becoming the person I knew you could be–"

I nod, not sure where to look.

He sighs. "Well," he says, "I guess it's time to explain why I left and what happened just before I did."

I get that cold feeling again. "Maybe you shouldn't," I say. "Maybe we should leave it alone for now. I mean, there's no way to go back and fix things. Whatever we do now, we can never get back the lost time. The only thing we can do is decide how we want to move forward."

He shakes his head. "I left you guys knowing that your mom would end up handling things *her* way. And I knew her way wasn't going to work, either. Not in the long run. I think maybe, looking back, I should've pushed more."

"But you didn't," I say.

"I didn't," he agrees. "But it's not over, Willow. It's not like we passed that station and now it doesn't matter anymore."

"But it doesn't."

The waitress brings up our bill. The place is starting to fill up, students and brief-cased wannabees flock to the few empty tables. I guess the waitress wants to free up ours.

"I know a guy," my dad says. "He's a professional. He's the one who helped get back to…" he gestures vaguely. "To whatever normalcy I now enjoy." He smiles. "It took me a long time to find him, to find the right guy with the right approach." He thinks it over. "He's a bit like you, actually. He understands that most solutions are actually about finding the right way to look at a problem. Once you look at a problem the right way, the rest kind of falls into place."

"What's he got to do with me?"

"Even as a little girl you'd always talk things through with these pro and con voices in your head. Well, talking to this guy is more like talking to you than anyone else I know, so maybe you could talk to him. He could help you adjust your way of looking at things."

Dad is starting to ramble.

I don't need help. I don't need to run my thoughts past any more voices, external or internal.

"You probably should've been seeing him from the beginning," Dad says, "but I only found him a little while ago. All the other guys I tried, they were no good for me. They just made things worse."

He slides a business card across the table.

The way chloe did.

Decades ago.

I think back over the last few months. Struggling to find the right way to connect with SSJ Bailey. Creating a new channel to help me decode the intricate male-female dance. Helping my followers with my posts and then seeing chloe misconstrue my advice and still end up with a guy – *my* guy. Evil-Cyrano-ing my channel and almost losing all my serious followers. Starting on my heart-ache cure, putting myself out there, meeting up with my followers, making friends, talking to new people and even, little by little, re-connecting with Dad. And I find myself wondering how much easier all that might have been if I didn't have to do it alone. If I didn't have to come up with every single answer by myself.

I could've used someone insightful and experienced by my side, giving me advice for a change.

I pick up the card and flip it over. Feel its texture, its density, the raised lettering. I'm not sure I'll take this card home with me. I'm not sure I'll ever use the number on the back. But, if I'm truthful, something about this doesn't feel completely wrong. Even if it doesn't feel completely right, either.

"He's just a guy," Dad says. "All he does is talk. Talk and listen. That doesn't sound too bad, does it?"

That's true. I'm nothing if not a fan of words.

"And," he says, "who knows, you might end up helping him more than he helps you. You have that kind of effect on people."

39

Back at work I'm dismayed to find that my computer has crashed. For no quantifiable reason, while it was merely sleeping until my return, it still managed to execute a command so thoroughly confusing it had no option but to commit temporary suicide.

I restart the thing while I go back over my conversation with Dad. For all his beating around the bush, he did make a few good points. On the other hand, that doesn't mean I should just forget about the ancient wisdom of *letting sleeping dogs lie*. After all, that particular insight probably evolved over centuries, saving millions of lives in the process. You don't just throw out that kind of ancient wisdom after a quick lunch conversation.

My computer starts up but immediately hangs again. It shows a progress bar that is clearly not progressing. Not even very, very slowly. I watch it for a full minute, just to make sure. It's not.

Desperate, I switch the thing off completely, pull its cord from the wall, and let it sit for another minute to think about what it's done.

I really don't need all this electronic drama right now. I don't want to deal with people coming to fix my computer and, perchance, looking at my browser history and my Keep pages.

That's way too dangerous.

I plug the machine back in and this time it starts up correctly. A wave of relief washes over me.

Of course, it still refuses to tell me what was wrong before or why it's being so compliant now, but at least my browser history is safe. I clear it just to be sure.

The afternoon drags on and when I finally get home there's only the slightest hint of mom-ness about the place. There are vague traces of her perfume, distant sounds of vacuuming, and wisps of echoes of her trek through our domicile, but it's all very subtle, very ethereal.

I don't go looking for her, either. I know how difficult it is for her not to jump on me the second I arrive, so she must be working at top capacity to stay at the fringes of my perception. Moreover, I have other problems to deal with. For one thing, there's Melissa Moretti, my wayward childhood friend, who's just opened my front door for me and now wants to take my coat.

"I hope you don't mind," she says. "I just popped over to see how you were doing. Your mom said it'd be okay to wait inside."

"Great," I say, feeling instantly nervous and seriously considering running back to my car and driving around until Melissa either expires, or goes back home.

She smiles at me patiently, waiting for my coat, and I wonder when we entered this 'just popping over unannounced' phase in our relationship.

"You could've just emailed," I say, handing over my coat.

"Sure," she says, "but we live close, so…"

"Or sent me a text. Or left me a comment. Or just imagined how I was, and left it at that."

Melissa laughs as if none of those are actually viable options.

"I brought some Tamagotchis," she says, excitedly.

I eye her suspiciously. "Do you mean Tamagotchis to play with or Tamagotchis to leave in their original packaging so we can admire them as collectibles?"

"Tamagotchis to leave in their original packaging so we can admire them as collectibles," she says quickly.

"Oh." I try to remember what a normal person would do at this precise moment, and something actually surfaces. "I would offer you some tea," I tell her, "but Mom's the only one who can work the fidgety water cooker and she seems to be fringing at the moment."

"Fringing?" Melissa gives me a look. "What's that?"

"I'm not too sure myself. It's this new thing she's trying. It's pretty complicated but the only immediate impact is that there will be no tea."

"That's fine," Melissa says. "I brought juice boxes."

Which is very confusing. She starts to laugh. "Relax," she says. "I was only joking."

We head into the living room and Melissa takes two Tamagotchis from her bag. They're indeed mint in box and she places them on the table. We admire them for a while and I'm surprised how little I care about these toys. Even less than I imagined I would. But I also get a sense of what they mean to Melissa. This is not just about her dipping her toe into the nostalgia pool. This is about her reconnecting with something from her past and preserving it for her future.

After a few minutes she starts to speak, but instead of reminiscing about the toys, she tells me about her boyfriend and their breakup.

"So now," she says, "after a few months, I've decided to start dating again. I mean, I'm not looking for a long-term relationship just yet, but I want to get out of the house and start talking to guys, you know?"

I happy to be back on some familiar ground. "Of course," I say. "Dopamine must flow, however small the trickle."

"Sure," she says, not really listening. "So I made a profile on a dating site and, out of the blue, my ex starts sending me messages again. And then he starts dropping by, checking the oil and tires on my car and things. What do you think that means?"

I mull this over. "Do you think it's possible he found your dating profile?"

Melissa shrugs. "Could be," she says, "but why would that matter? He broke up with me, right? Why does he care if I'm dating again?"

She turns the Tamagotchis over so we can admire the other side of the packaging for a while. "The problem is," she says, "it's way too confusing. Am I supposed to delete my profile and give him another chance? Is that what he wants? And, if so, why doesn't he say so?"

"I think maybe you're looking at this the wrong way," I tell her. "Why are you waiting for him to make that decision?"

"How do you mean?"

"Instead of waiting for him to make up his mind, which he may never actually do, just make your own decision. Decide what kind of life you want, and then start working towards it."

"I suppose I should," she says, "but it'd be so much easier if he came back, you know? If we could just pick up where we left off?"

"Of course it'd be easier," I say. "But even if he did want you back, how long would that last? How long before whatever made him leave the first time starts nagging at him again? How long before he starts looking around for other options? Do you really want to live your life walking on eggshells, hoping you don't say or do the wrong thing? Hoping no one else catches his eye?"

Melissa picks up one of the boxes without really looking at it. "You know what?" she says. "You're right. You're absolutely right. That's not the life I want. I deserve better. I deserve to choose for myself."

"There you go."

I'm not a complete idiot. I know this isn't going to be easy for her. She has a lot of work to do and most of it is going to be an immense struggle, but at least she knows where she's going now. and why.

She looks back at me. "So," she says, "you want to open these babies and see if we can keep them alive for an hour?"

"Sure," I say. "Why not."

It's dark when Melissa leaves. I head up to my studio but don't feel like making a new post just yet. I don't have the energy and my mind is still preoccupied with everything that has happened today.

I dig in my pockets for the business card Dad gave me. Maybe I should dial that number, you know, just to make sure it's still in service.

40

So this guy blowing his nose and surreptitiously checking the results isn't the real therapist.

He's probably just the assistant, in charge of inviting you in, asking if you need anything (some water, maybe?), and doing the intake interview.

But the intake interview has gone on for a while now and the questions are getting oddly specific (What are some of the things you'd like to work on? When would you say was the last time you were truly happy?) I shrug at these last two questions and ask him when I'm going to see the real therapist. He gives me an odd look and writes something down.

I'm starting to worry, actually At this rate, there won't be any time left for the real therapist to talk to me, figure out what's wrong, and say the magic words to fix me so I can go off happy.

Or whatever it is we're doing here.

"Could you tell me what your short-term goals are for these sessions? Have you thought about that?"

"I haven't. I guess I'll discuss it with the real therapist when he gets here."

"And what makes you feel that I'm not, as you put it, a 'real' therapist?"

Probably the fact that he doesn't look very therapist-y. And doesn't sound very therapisty. And doesn't act very therapisty. In short, he doesn't inspire any kind of therap-i-ness.

I tell him so.

He writes down 'therapiness,' then says, "Do you think you tend to overanalyze things? Maybe as a way of avoiding certain issues or thoughts?"

"Probably not, no. Why would you say that?"

"For one thing, you've spent more time looking at my shoes than my face. Why do you think that is?"

Why? Because those are not therapisty shoes. Those are the kind of shoes you wear to keep your feet warm while you're trying to decide whether you're going on a mud-run or you're going to paint the house.

"And why do you think it's so important to you that the 'real' therapy session hasn't started?"

That's actually a good question, and the irony isn't entirely lost on me. I feel hostile towards this man even though he isn't the real therapist. That doesn't make sense. Instead of being relieved I am actually pissed. Maybe it's because he's pushing so hard for me to mistake him for the therapist. It's like someone asking you how old they look. You just know they want you to be wrong by at least a decade.

That's way too much pressure.

But maybe opening up a little to this assistant isn't such a bad idea. Not being an actual therapist he might be less judgy, less formal. He won't have the answers any more than I do, so it'll be like talking to a normal mortal.

Just another almost-person like myself.

"I assume you know I've been talking to your father?"

"I do, but I'm pretty sure you're not supposed to mention that in any way, shape, or form."

He shoots me a little got-ya smile. "Are you calling me a real therapist now?" Then his face softens. "I'm allowed to mention it, actually. I just can't give you any details about his sessions. And you can feel safe that I won't share any of your details either. But I can tell you that your father has given me some of your family background."

"Has he now." I'm starting to worry again. When do we get to the part where I'm helping him more than he's helping me? Where he realizes that I'm freakishly intelligent and he should be asking *me* for advice? That's the only bit I'm looking forward to.

I guess it comes later.

"Do you mind if we talk about your family?" He turns up the air-conditioning without moving. "I'd like to get your take on things."

I hug my jumper. "There's no point," I tell him. "There's nothing to tell."

"You currently live with your mother?"

"I don't," I huff. "She lives with me."

"In her house, right?"

"I guess if you're desperate to be historically accurate, then yes, it was originally her house."

"What about your father? He tells me he was absent for a large part of your childhood."

"He has… issues."

"I guess that's a fair assessment. Can you think of any other people with issues?"

I shrug. "I think most people on the planet have issues. It's a very common theme."

"Okay. What about your mother, would you say she has issues?"

"That's difficult to say."

"Why's that?"

"It's just hard to tell where the issues end and my mother begins."

He smiles at this. "Okay," he says, "I could see that. Anybody else we should talk about?"

"Me?" I roll my eyes at him. "No, I don't have issues."

"Alright, let's park that for the moment. Anybody else?"

I suddenly feel unsteady. Not just cold, but a little dizzy too. I should've asked for something to drink after all.

"Anybody at all, Willow?"

"I don't think so."

A glass of water appears in my hand. The non-therapist sits back in his chair. I take a careful sip, not sure how I managed to lose that bit of time.

"Is that better?"

"Sure," I say. "I'm okay."

Although grueling, eventually the session does end. There are no magic words to fix me with, of course, unless you count the words, 'see you next time', but I feel those are more like magic-money-making words for the therapist himself. Nevertheless, I make a little pact with myself to see this thing through, at least for a little while. There's no point going through all this and then quitting just before I reap any benefits.

So back I go the following week, and the one after that, and the one after that.

Low and behold, the sessions do become easier. That is to say, it takes less mental effort to force myself to drive over to his office and opening up to the man starts to feel like second nature.

In a way – yet again – I probably see the sessions as some kind of separate dimension, the therapist as a virtual being: nothing I do in that office can intrude on my real world. The therapist, after all, is bound by professional ethics to never repeat anything I say. So, in a way, my words go right into a void, waiting, I suppose for that void to eventually pop out some kind of answer.

So far, though, no luck.

This therapist very much seems to be about asking questions and at times I wonder if he's ever even heard of the concept of answers.

Mom does ask a question or two from time to time, but she's careful never to scratch the surface. It's always just, 'how are the sessions going,' or, 'are you sure you'll be on time?' No follow up questions. No details. No discussions. Which is exactly how I like it.

But, on some level, I do feel a change. The sessions are slowly but surely going deeper. The topics getting more serious and the level of detail going up. My own reactions seem to be intensifying also. It's almost as if he's trying to ease me into something. Building me up for a charge against some end-level boss.

I have no idea how true this actually is until, one day, the sessions take another dip into further depths.

Looking back over his notes, the therapist says, "The first time you came in I asked if there were other people you'd like to talk about. We then discussed your mom, your dad, and yourself. Today I'd like to talk to you about someone else."

My heckles are suddenly up. "Who?"

"I'd like to talk about your older sister, is that okay?"

Like it did in the first session, the temperature in the room suddenly drops. By a full ten degrees this time. It almost makes me gasp.

"Your father mentioned you two were very close."

I try to wrap my mind around his words but I feel confused, panicky, betrayed. Is this guy really going there? Doesn't he know I'm alone? Doesn't he know I've always been alone and I always will be?

"She was older than you." He checks his notes. "Two years older, almost to the day?"

I can't talk.

"She was eleven and you were nine?"

"I don't really– Maybe..."

"That's what your father told me."

"I guess..."

"What was her name?"

I take a sip of water. The dizziness is back and I feel lightheaded, too. As if I might float away – a little puff of Willow-consciousness going for a stroll outside her body.

"Alice," I hear myself say. "My big sister's name was Alice."

"Good." The therapist makes a couple of notes. I'm not sure if he's really writing or just doodling. I try to get back to my body but I'm still too floaty.

"She sounds wonderful. Can you tell me what Alice looked like?"

My mind floats away on over my memories. I haven't seen photos of Alice in years. I may never have seen photos. Someone must have hidden them. But do recall some things, now that I allow my mind to go there. It's more like feelings than images, though. With Alice there was always friendliness, caring, protection. There was lots of explaining, lots of planning and building. Always being together, always looking out for each other.

There were long ago summers, walking in the woods. I can see a flash of dark hair, an orange jumper, some freckles and a never-ending smile.

We'd lug around a fallen tree to make a bridge, or collect shiny stones, or go swimming in a creek.

The images are vague and mixed up, nothing in chronological order.

"Do you think part of you is angry with Alice for leaving?"

I'm suddenly back in the room, cold and empty and angry. "Yes!" I blurt out. "She was supposed to do this *with* me. We were supped to help each other!" I feel my nails digging into my palms. "This is a horribly mean world and she swore we'd figure it out together!"

"Good," the therapist says. "It's okay to be angry."

"It's not. I don't want to be angry. I never want to be angry with Alice, but I am and I can't help it."

"It wasn't fair," he says. "You didn't deserve what happened and neither did she."

"She promised me she'd never leave!"

"But it didn't work out that way."

My water is gone. The therapist gets up and pours me some more.

"That's the way the world works sometimes," he says. "We don't always get fair. We don't always get what's coming to us. It doesn't matter how good or kind or wonderful we are, we just get what we get."

I try to follow what he's saying.

"When things like that happen, it can shut us down, makes us numb to our emotions. Or we decide that we can't trust anyone anymore. And why would we? Whenever we confide in someone, they eventually end up leaving us, so what's the point?"

"There is no point," I agree.

"Maybe," he says. "But I don't think our lives are meant to be perfect. And I don't think it's our job to try and make them perfect, either. All we have to do is find ways to deal with the things that come our way so we can keep going and feel good at least some of the time."

I finish the water and ask for more. He empties the jug into my glass. "Look, Willow," he says, "there are many ways of doing that. Many ways of dealing with things. Some good, some not so good, and some really bad." He gives me a sad smile. "And you had to figure out a way all on your own, didn't you?"

"I did."

"You were only nine years old at the time. That seems like a pretty tall order for a little girl, don't you think?"

He's right. Even though I'm pretty intelligent in many unexpected ways, that was probably a lot for me to handle.

"I know you did the best you could, but that was a long time ago. Do you think that now, together, we could come up with an even better way?" He gives me an encouraging smile. "Would you be willing to try something a little more comfortable?"

That sounds good, in theory, but I wouldn't know how. I'm all out of ideas. "I don't even know where to start," I tell him.

"Well," he says, "maybe you can start by talking to Alice again?"

"Talk to her?"

The therapist nods. "Here's what I want you to do…"

Video #99 by *Kayleigh*. **Views: 27**

Comments:

MandyGirl26: (7:15 pm) Where did Kayleight go?

ChloeGirl: (8:07 pm) No post in weeks, something's wrong!

Hopegone72: (10:19 pm) Longest radio silence since the beginning of this channel!

AnnyT: (10:22 pm) K, I have big problem. Please come help me!

Allof12: (11:03 pm) It doesn't matter, she never even understood the fundamental difference between men and women, which is that women never really grow out of playing with dolls. They just get a little taller and continue playing dress up with themselves. They become their own dolls. Follow my channel <u>here</u>.

Minnie12: (11:55 pm) You got that all wrong, dude! Women are like horses: you can't appear nervous around them or youll scare them off. They have to feel that you're in control and know exactly what you're doing. That they're safe around you. That's why you need to exude confidence at all times.

GettingThereSlowly: (11:56 pm) Did you just call me a horse!!??? Dude!!??

Minnie12: (11:57 pm) Nope. Learn to read, I said 'like', as in sharing a single common property with something. Duh.

AnnyT: (12:11 pm) Stop trying to steal K's followers! You people are dirty vultures. We don't even know what happened to K!

Hopegone72: (12:16 pm) We get that you believe in the illusion of scarcity, in allowing people to miss you and everything, but it's time to come back, K.

<h1 style="text-align:center">41</h1>

I've never been what you might call a connoisseur of silences – I've always found them awkward and wasteful – but I've come to appreciate the need for a well-placed silence now and again, and there's definitely a need now, which is why I've let the current silence go on uninterrupted for so long. However, there comes a point where you have to ask yourself if you're still dealing with a silence or whether all communication has simply stopped.

"So," I say, "It's good to see you two here today. I'm really proud you came." I give them each an encouraging nod. "And I'm even more proud that you've stayed so long."

More silence.

"This isn't easy," I go on. "It can't be easy, but please don't give up."

The silence drags on. I'm not sure whether this is a new silence or just the continuation of the previous silence. Although I've just spoken, the silence between the two of them is still intact, so I guess I haven't really broken it at all.

The last few days were extra rough. Starting with my first visit to the therapist, which left my brain reeling, trying to piece together a new and coherent way of looking at things, and continuing with the therapist's exercise, and another exercise that I gave myself.

But there were some highlights. For instance, Gary discovered that many of the brilliant reports he'd attributed to my co-workers were actually mine. That was a nice surprise. Although I don't need his approval, or even want it, it can't hurt to have my brilliance recognized from time to time. So work has been slightly less of a bare-ass trip down the cheese grater.

And my channel has begun to recover from all the Evil-Cyrano crap I pulled. The comments from my real followers are starting to outweigh those of the comedy hunters, and that's definitely a good sign. I'm not sure I'll fully reclaim my reputation as a serious video blogger, but things do seem to be looking up. Sadly, I haven't had time to make more videos. The exercise the therapist gave me has kept me pretty busy. And right now I'm working on a new exercise, too, one that I gave myself.

"Why don't you guys tell each other what it's like to be in the same room again?"

Mom shoots me a worried look, but I urge nod for her to go for it.

"Well," she says softly. "I think…. I think you look like yourself."

I'm not entirely sure what that means, but at least she's shattered the silence.

Dad nods and says "Yeah, you too."

Which is a start. I let out a little sigh of relief. This could have gotten so much worse.

Mom was pretty upset about coming home and finding Dad on our couch. I guess the reverse-ambush thing isn't that much fun. I fully believe that this serves a higher purpose, though, so I'm okay with doing this to her.

For his part, Dad was surprised at my request for him to come over, but he didn't put up a fight. In fact, he arrived within ten minutes. We were talking about his life and his job when Mom returned from her knitting club.

"You look, the same," Mom goes on, her voice still fragile. "I mean, you look older, but I can still see it's you."

"You too," Dad says again.

I give him a little nudge. "That's good, but maybe you could elaborate more?"

"Well," he says, "it's like I still know it's her, even though I don't really know her. I mean, we've all changed, it's been so long, but at the same time it still feels familiar."

Mom nods as if that makes sense to her.

"So," she says, "this is where Willow and I live now."

Dad makes a point of looking around, even though he's been here since an hour before Mom's return. "It's nice," he says.

"It's not," Mom says, "but thank you for saying so."

Another silence and I immediately fear the worst, but then Dad says, "I've been here before, you know. Not in the house of course, but I've been in the street, outside."

Mom considers this for a moment. "Well," she says, "maybe you should've come inside."

Dad looks at me, then back at her. "Should I have?"

Mom shrugs. She's not sure.

The two of them handled Alice's departure very differently. I don't think either of them went about it the right way, but I don't necessarily believe they went about it the wrong way, either. They just did the best they could at the time. Mom trying to bury the pain in the past, pretending Alice never existed, Dad running away and giving us room for whatever he thought would happen without him. But what we're doing here today is not about second-guessing or placing blame, it's about trying out something new. Something different.

This is like a reset.

"So Dad," I say, trying to pre-shatter another oncoming silence, "why don't you tell Mom about some of the things you've been up to?"

Dad raises an eyebrow, then starts talking.

I'm not an idiot, I know we're not going to come out of this a normal, happy family. That's not in the cards for us. Dad isn't going to move back in, Mom isn't going to forget he left, and none of us can ignore the years we lost or the hole we carry deep inside. But I do think things will change. From here on in, things will be different. Maybe in big ways, but probably in many small ways, at least in the beginning. Either way, things are definitely going to change.

I head to the kitchen to get them some tea.

There's a strange full-circle-ness to this situation. Years ago I was the little girl holding mini-lectures in the living room, surprising her parents with her strange ways of looking at the world, and now I've grown into my thoughts, into my brain, and we're back here, with me trying to fix them.

I feel very.... real.

When I return with the drinks, I'm happy to see they're still talking, if somewhat cryptic and haphazardly. I decide to leave them to it. This next part has nothing to do with me, and I have my own work to do. I have my own journey to concentrate on.

I take my coat and head to the mall for my next step.

42

I notice I feel much less trepidation than I usual do when I approach the nut store. Or I feel a different kind of trepidation. Normally, just before entering, my heart rate spikes, my breath catches, and a panicky voice starts telling me I'm not fully prepared. But today I only feel a kind of foreboding, as if I'm heading into a rainstorm. It's going to be unpleasant, yes, but it's unlikely to kill me.

"Hey!" Bailey says as I walk in. "There she is! Where have you been?"

I wave a little hello as I approach the counter. Bailey is wearing a big grin that tells me he's really happy about something. I can't tell whether it's seeing me or just his life in general. There's a sparkle in his eyes when we make eye-contact, though. Then again, I could just be imagining that.

"You finally ran out of Brazils?"

"It appears so."

I feel like I haven't seen Bailey in an eternity. Forever squared. And I feel a little elated, too, as if I'm running into a long lost childhood friend, or a very minor celebrity. Someone who's instantly familiar but also strange and otherworldly.

"So, what can I get you? A hundred grams like always?"

"No, that's okay," I say. "No need to go all the way to the back for the Brazils. I'll just have some regular cashews."

Bailey gives me a look. "Regular cashews? Really?"

"Sure. Sometimes the exotic just looks more fun but isn't all that healthy for you."

Bailey laughs, and, for a brief moment, I have to remind myself that I have no feelings for him – other than, perhaps, some slight animosity.

"I know you're joking," he says, touching my arm for a second. "There's no way Willow comes all the way to a specialty nut store just to get some boring old cashews."

Animosity for making me waste so much of my time.

"They're only boring if you've had too many," I point out. "And I haven't had cashews in a long time."

"No problem," he says. "I always thought the peppered Brazils were pretty disgusting, to be honest."

"Guess it took me longer than most to find out."

My voice sounds a little shaky. Must be all that animosity.

Although I'm not sure why animosity makes my heart beat a little faster whenever he smiles at me.

"We're still talking about nuts, aren't we?" Bailey says, still smiling.

"Because you sound very serious."

I shrug. "Of course we are."

"So, what happened?" He scoops up cashews that no-one will ever eat. "You haven't been by the store, you haven't responded to my messages, I was starting worry."

"Nothing happened. I was just busy. There were all these people who needed, things I had to do. It kind of slipped my mind, you know? Sorry about that."

"Well," he says, a little baffled, "I wish you'd unslip your mind, because I really missed you."

Which is what I've wanted him to say for so long.

But I don't anymore.

Do I?

Either way, he's not fooling me. I know that by *'I really missed you,'* he simply means that he's noticed I wasn't around. Which is a little late in the game and doesn't mean all that much.

Bailey checks the clock. "Hey, I have a break coming up, let's get a coffee." He smiles mischievously. "We can talk about your plane and my building. It'll be fun."

"I'd love to," I say, "but I can't. I have way too much to do."

"Come on," he says. "You don't want me to think you're angry with me, do you?" He winks at me and I'm surprised at how little this affects me.

"Don't worry," I say. "It's nothing like that. I just have things to do."

And if I said yes, you'd just take out your cell and invite chloe along.

Because you're probably still together.

Which also doesn't really matter.

"Alright," he says. "But you have to promise me you'll reply to my messages, okay? I miss our little chats."

I shrug noncommittally as Bailey hands me the cashews, touching my hand a little longer than necessary.

When I step back out of the store I feel a little empty, but it's not the emptiness I used to feel when Bailey and I parted. That feeling of an invisible cord stretching out between us, fighting to snap us back together. Right now there's just a dim sense of something being over, and I realize how relieved this makes me feel. How liberating it is. As if I've been released from some kind of evil spell.

I'm an ex-prisoner soaking up sunlight for the first time in years.

I'm free!

I'm so happy I don't have to go home and spend hours pining for Bailey, obsessively analyzing everything he's just said and planning our next interaction.

I don't *have* to do anything right now. Which is great. It saves so much time.

As I pass the food court, I suddenly feel weird, like I'm being watched. It's an unfamiliar sensation because I usually feel invisible. I try to shrug it off but I can't. For some reason I'm absolutely sure someone, somewhere, is looking at me.

I scan the tables and, at first glance, no one stands out. It takes me two more slow scans to notice another, mostly invisible person giving me a look. It's a bland looking guy who's putting on weight and dresses like even his mother gave up on him ever having a social life. It's the dopamine guy. The one who asked me if I smoked and drank cats. I give him a friendly nod.

He gives me the finger and leaves.

I smile. I'm going to be okay, and so is he.

As I head to my car, I marvel at the debilitating properties of unrequited love. How easily it can consume all of your time and energy, holding your every thought hostage.

You only notice this when you pop out the other end, of course, when you finally stop waiting for your crush to grant you a second of his time.

Right now I feel silly for having been that girl. The one who was so debilitatingly in love with a guy who clearly wasn't into her.

I still don't know exactly what I'm going to do with the rest of my life. I still want to find someone to share it with. But now I'm free to choose. It doesn't *have* to be Bailey. In fact, I don't *want* it to be Bailey.

I take a moment to let that thought sink in.

I honestly don't want it to be Bailey.

I get into my car and drive to my last appointment of the day.

There's a final trap I need to warn you about. Because, just when you think you're going to be okay, that you're completely over your crush, he's going to try to pull you back in.
Oh yes, he will.
Escaped prisoners are always hunted down.

[hold up chart #1]

Maybe he'll flash you that cool smile that you fell in love with. Or he'll remind you of all the fun you had. He might even touch your arm and look deep into your eyes. ~~And, even if he doesn't do any of this consciously, he'll do it all the same, and always for the same reason. And this reason is not that he suddenly realizes how wonderful you are. Not that he just needed to miss you to understand how perfect you two would be together. Nope, it's not that at all.~~

He'll do this just to see if he *can*.
He wants to know that he still has power over you. That he still has you as a backup-chick if things don't work out for him.

He's like a child losing his least favorite toy: even though he doesn't play with it, he doesn't want anyone else to play with it, either. And he knows, subconsciously, how nice it is to have someone pining for away him. It's a great confidence booster. And when that feeling disappears, he misses IT. But that doesn't mean he misses YOU.

Be warned, the only thing on offer here is for you to come back into his life in a very, very small way. He wants you back in your old, painful role, waiting around, doting over his every message. And make no mistake, if you let him, he'll keep this up for years. No time limit to this has ever been established.

So what can you, as someone using my list, do about this? Well, think of this as a test. Your final exam.

[hold up chart #2]

And how do you know when you've passed this exam? For one thing, you're not actually over him until you stop secretly wanting him back. You're not over him until he could give you a perfectly reasonable explanation for your 'break-up', show you that it was all just a misunderstanding and that he still 'loves' you, and you still wouldn't take him back.

Anything less and you're just kidding yourself...

When you don't need him (or anyone else) to fix your life for you, when you can be happy on your own, that's when you're ready. So tell me, are you going to graduate today, or are you going to cave and take his whole damn course over again?

[sign off]

So that was my final exam, Alice, and I'm happy to report that I passed.

Okay, maybe I didn't pass with flying colors. Maybe not with any great lengths to spare, but I still did it. He tried to pull me back in and I resisted. I battled his looks and his smile and all of his offers valiantly, until I was free.

Of course, at that point I still wasn't sure what I was going to do next. I wasn't sure what to do with my channel, with the oceans of time ahead of me, or even with my dad. But, well, that's just life. There's never a single moment when all of your problems are solved. There's always ongoing stuff. Like this new journey I'm now on, working on the therapist's exercise.

So I hope you'll stick around, Alice.

Because there's more to come.

Epilogue

I'm on my way to this little restaurant at the end of the pier. Anatova's sent me a string of messages about a life or death situation, and, although with Anatova this could mean just about anything, I'm not taking any chances with the lives of my followers.

I arrive to find her sitting in the back, tearing up an innocent coaster. Despite her age, she jumps out of her seat when she sees me and pulls me up a chair.

"K!" she beams. "You actually came!"

Worry melts from her face.

"Of course I did."

I take a seat and Anatova drops back into hers, her giant frame making the chair all but squeal. "It's been so long," she says. "I think maybe you disappear forever. No update for weeks, no meet-ups. What is going on?"

She's right. I've been so busy with my new journey that I've completely neglected my channel. To be honest, I didn't think anyone would care. I expected my followers to quietly disappear. After all, the internet is home to thousands of people willing to dish out free dating advice.

"I've been writing," I tell Anatova.

She's elated. "More YouTube scripts?"

"No, actually. I'm writing a book."

"This is great news! Book from the great Kayleigh! This is what world needs. When can I read?"

"I'm sorry, it's not that kind of book." I do my best to temper her enthusiasm. It's important she understands I'm taking this particular journey alone. Or mostly alone. I do get some training-wheel-like help from my therapist, and I've had some surprisingly candid talks with my parents.

"It's more of an exercise," I tell her.

"Oh?"

"A *personal* exercise," I add quickly. "I'm writing to my big sister. Telling her about everything she's missed. Like what I'm up to now, why I set up my channel, how that backfired and got me working on what could be the greatest of all human problems… that kind of thing." I think a moment, then add, "I even mention meeting you and my other followers."

"Really? I am in secret book by Kayleigh? That is wonderful!"

"It *is* wonderful. At least for me. It's very cathartic, makes me feel like my big sister is still on this journey with me, you know?"

"Da," Anatova looks away for a moment, her face hardening slightly. "I also had big sister," she says. "We were good in beginning, like best friends, but then I move here, to this country, and we almost lose touch." She wipes something invisible from her face. "We make visit not long ago," she says. "As it turned out, it was only just in time."

She looks back at me. "Is good to keep communicating, K," she says. "Any way you can."

I take a breath. "Yeah. It took me a while to figure that out."

Anatova examines my face. "You know, your sister would be very proud of you. I am sure of this. You are very good person."

"I hope so...."

I'm not sure where to look. Thankfully a waitress comes to take our order. I ask her to bring me some tea, Anatova orders a substantial collection of beers.

"Any-of-way," Anatova says, "I have also news. And I have many, many life-or-death questions."

"So I gathered."

"Da. You maybe will not believe," she says, "but I meet wonderful American male on site called Facebook." She pauses to gauge my reaction. "Have you heard of this Facebook?"

I nod. "I'm quite familiar with it. I think most breathing humans are."

"Okay, well, Facebook is new for me. I am getting good with Tube, but I did not hear of Facebook. My neighbor set up account for me. Is really cool."

"Good for you."

"Any-of-way, I was minding my own business, not putting nose into anything, just like good Russian woman, simply clicking 'like' on picture of surfer, then, suddenly, there is Stan, asking to be friend."

Anatova shakes her head in remembered amazement.

"Can you imagine this? Stan and I become friends through internet! I mean, how often that happens?"

"Well, probably just about all the time."

Anatova's enthusiasm falters. "Why do you say this?"

"To be honest, it doesn't mean that much to be someone's friend on Facebook. It's like... winning a paper medal, which was left out in the rain, and has someone else's name on it. It's nice but not all that special."

Anatova waves it away. "You are thinking of other internet-book, K," she says. "Stan and I are very serious about our relationship."

"Your *relationship*? Anatova, how many friends do you have on Facebook?"

Anatova is shocked. "One, of course. Only Stan. I am not insensitive playgirl!"

"Just one?" I take a moment to digest this. "You do realize most

Facebook users have hundreds of friends, right? Some have thousands. Facebook friends are not considered a big deal."

"No, no," Anatova insists. "Stan and I have special relationship. He even make pictures of his abs appear on my computer. He is very smart."

"That happens automatically. That's what Facebook does."

"I don't think so."

I take out my cell and ask her for Stan's full name. It only takes me a second to find him. "Is this the guy?"

Anatova checks my cell. "Da!" she says, excited. "That is my man. He is great, don't you think?"

"Sure, I guess. But isn't he a bit young?"

Anatova shrugs. "He is older than he looks, that is not good picture. He already become seventeen on last birthday."

"Seventeen? I don't even think that's legal."

"I think it is, K."

"I'm pretty sure it's not. In fact, I don't even think you're supposed to call him a man, technically."

Anatova gets a bit crabby. "Look," she says, "this is whole new age, K. Generation X is very progressive, they don't care about artificial boundaries like age and heritage. And Stan sends me all day messages. He doesn't go to store without telling Anatova. He doesn't brush teeth without sending Anatova picture of brush, and sometimes of abs. And he is so excited when he writes Anatova that he forgets even to use vowels. This is real thing, I know."

I click around Stan's profile. "Generation X was over thirty years ago," I tell Anatova, treading a little more carefully now. I don't like where this is going, but I can't leave Anatova in this weird little dream world. It wouldn't be fair. Someone has to wake her up.

"They're not really messages, they're public posts, and it just saves time to leave out some obvious vowels." I show her my cell again. "Did you even check his personal details?"

"Of course not!" Anatova looks appalled. "I am not insensitive stalker-girl!"

"But you should *always* check profile details. They're public, see? Even I can see them. You're supposed to look at them. See this number right here, for instance?"

Reluctantly, Anatova glances at my cell.

"Number 1782?"

"Yes. That's his number of friends."

Anatova is confused. "How do you mean?"

"I mean, you are just 1 of his 1782 friends."

"That can't be. We are special together. Your phone is not doing that right. You are supposed to do that on computer, not phone."

I suppress a sigh. "Okay, fine. Let's assume that the number got mangled somehow. Now let's look at his Relationship Status, it says here he's dating someone."

"It does?" Anatova pipes up again. "You think he means me?"

"No, Anatova, I do not. In fact, any time you even have to ask that question, the answer is probably 'No'."

She frowns. "Well, he could be sending me hint or something…"

"He could," I agree, "but let's pretend we live in the real world for a moment, shall we?"

Anatova shrugs.

"I know this isn't nice to hear, I know it stings, but I honestly believe this Stan-thing is a dead end. I'm really, really sorry."

"So you sure? There is not maybe still small chance?"

"I'm sorry, Anatova. If he's even aware of your existence, then you're just a friend to him. And an internet friend at that."

Anatova sighs. Something seems to finally click in her head and she slumps back in her seat. This wasn't fun to do, but it had to be done, and the sooner the better.

I signal the waitress to bring us something stronger to drink. We're going to be here a while and my Russian friend is way too sober to start any kind of healing process.

I look over at her, at her hardened, time-worn features, and I can almost see her slip into that dark hole. I can almost sense her letting go of the life she'd planned out for her and Stan.

"What can I do, K?" she asks, her voice sounding fragile for the first time since I met her.

"Don't worry," I tell her. "You're not alone. I'm here and I'm going to help you. I know exactly what to do."

After all, I've come up with a killer cure for just this type of situation.

bailey: Sup? :)

bailey: Are you there, Willow?
bailey: I miss you…

bailey: Alright, I guess ur busy…

I'm so happy you made it this far. Obviously you're an amazingly resilient reader. Subscribe here to get your copy of 'Hermit Girl – The Lost Chapters':

thehermitgirl.blogspot.com

And pretty-please tell all your friends about this book, especially if you don't like them all that much and don't care what my weird writing will do to their brains. Novels disappear when people stop talking about them.

And, *and,* in the unlikely event you don't hate this novel and plan on burning it in a cleansing ritual, please leave a review.